AF229484

# THE STEP BEFORE DEATH

## JAMIE FRANCOIS

Make A Way Publications
Miami, Florida

This book is the work of fiction. The characters, incidents, dialogue and places are drawn from the author's imagination and are not to be construed as real. Any resemblance to actual events, companies, institutions, or persons, living or dead, is entirely coincidental.

Make A Way Publications
810 SW 102nd Terrace Unit 101
Pembroke Pines, Florida, 33025
Tel: (305) 988-7031
Email: makeawaypub@gmail.com

Book Layout & Design By: www.UrbanFictionEditor.com
Edited By: Mary McBeth



Step Before Death
First Edition

ISBN 13-digit 978-1-5323-4964-5


Library of Congress Control Number: 2017911570

# CONTENTS

# CHAPTER 1
# THE STEP BEFORE DEATH

"Nigga, you ready?" Ace asked his homeboy Black.

"Nigga you know I'm ready," responded Black.

"Okay! Let's go get this money." Ace and Black were preparing to rob a cell phone store they'd been eyeing for the past couple of weeks. The two were known for knocking over stores in the 305 and the Miami-Dade Police Department had been on their asses for a few months now.

They exited the all black Toyota Camry, their usual get-away car, and marched toward the front of the store. It was a bright mid-summer's day, but these two didn't give a fuck about the scenery, they were stone cold robbers. "Come on nigga! Catch up," Ace told Black as he struggled to keep pace. Black had been caught in a shoot out with the police during their last lick.

"Nigga you see I'm trying! This bullet in my leg hurt like SHIT!"

Ace was dressed in a black hoodie, Khaki cargo shorts, and Jordan sneakers. Black wore a hoodie that matched his name, jeans, and a run down pair of red and black Air Force Ones. As they approached the front of the store, a white Chevy Yukon pulled up with a male and female couple sitting inside. Ace and Black were always careful in how they carried out their robberies; they didn't want the couple in the Yukon to spot them entering the store. Ace and Black stood in the front of the store trying not to draw attention to themselves. "Damn why the fuck they just sitting there?" asked Black.

"Iunno nigga. Look like they eating burgers & fries and shit," replied Ace.

"Man fuck that, let's slide in," ordered Black.

"Nigga you crazy! I got this big ass shot gun in my pants. You wanna get caught?" asked Ace.

After thirty minutes of waiting, they grew impatient, "Man fuck that, we out!" Ace hissed. Black swung the door to the store open without hesitation and slipped right into his usual role. Six eyes greeted him with amazement as the clerk and two customers froze in disbelief.

"Get behind the register!" Ace demanded of the store clerk.

"YAAAAAAAA!!!!!!!" The woman screamed as she stared down the barrel of the shotgun. "Please don't kill me! You can have it all—phones, money, whatever!"

"Shut the fuck up," Black responded. "Put the money in the bag, stupid hoe!"

The couple tried to remain calm, but were visibly shaken. Ace demanded the couple get down and they quickly complied, laying with their faces to the ground, while Black collected all the money. "Bitch hurry up!" he yelled.

"You almost done?" Ace asked.

"Yeah nigga, I got all that. We out."

They pushed through the door headed for the Camry. "Ohh shit my leg!" yelled Black. Ace responded by telling him to and catch up.

Back at the store the couple jumped up and ran out to their car.

The man switched on a dashboard mounted walkie talkie and announced, "This is Sergeant Mack, and there has just been a robbery on 183rd and 2nd Avenue."

Officer Kelly Jones chimed in, "The two suspects are armed and dangerous. One suspect is about 6 feet tall, brown skin, wearing a black hoodie, khaki cargo pants, and white & turquoise shoes. The second suspect is about 5 foot 9 inches, black hoodie, jean pants, and black and red shoes," reported Officer Jones.

"We are in pursuit; they've entered an all black Toyota Camry heading west. We need back up," ordered Sergeant Mack.

"Get the fuck out the way!" Ace yelled to oncoming traffic.

"Nigga hurry up!" yelled his accomplice, looking out the back window for any police cars.

"Fuck that nigga," said Ace, angrily, "You wanna drive or you gon let me do this?".

"Drive to the hood, we'll lose them there," replied Black.

"Slow the vehicle down," blared from the speaker of a police car behind them. The duo didn't even notice the all white Impala behind them because it was an undercover cop.

"Ohh shit, what we gon do?" asked Black.

"Nigga chill, Imma lose them." Ace made a left then a right, only to run into a road block.

"Damn they got us," said Black.

"Shit me nigga, I'm gone," replied Ace as he grabbed the bag full of money.

"Nigga let's go!" Black jumped out running the opposite way of the road block. They ran and ran, jumping fence after fence.

Replying to the initial call, Officer Channing spotted them from his police car and called it in.

"They are coming up on 187$^{th}$ and 5$^{th}$ ave," he said Officer Channing, before trailing right behind them on foot.

"Ahh fuck damn," Black yelled. As Ace looked back, he witnessed Black on the floor holding his leg. He wanted to go back and help, but the officer was getting too close. "Lil Bra get up!" Ace yelled. Black tried to get up but the pain was too much to bear.

"Freeze, you lil fucker, put your hands where I can see them and don't move!" said Officer Channing.

"Oooh, my leg!" screamed Black.

"Who gives a shit? You want to go around robbing people, huh?" asked Channing.

"Man, fuck you," said Black.

"Okay we'll see who's fucking who when you go away to prison for the rest of your life, said Channing.

*For the rest of my life?* thought Black. Black was only 20 years old and the sounds of that threw him off his whole vibe.

"Chhh…this is Officer Channing," he said into his walkie-talkie. "I've got one suspect in custody."

"Chhh…good work," said Sgt. Mack. Let's meet at the squad car."

"Alright, Sir, on my way," replied Channing, cuffing Black and snatching him to his feet, half dragging the screaming black back to his vehicle.

"Well, well, well, what do we have here," said Mack.

"This lil guy is slower than a turtle, I scooped him off the floor after falling from jumping a fence," said Channing.

"Man fuck you. You really lucky I'm hurt or I would of left yo ass in the dust," said Black.

*Waap*! Sgt. Mack slapped Black in the face. "Shut up and start talking. Where's your friend?"

"I ain't got no friend," said Black. Black looked up at Sgt. Mack with a puzzled face. *What the hell?* thought Black.

"What? You see a ghost? Officers wear regular clothes too." Officer Channing and Sgt. Mack laughed as Officer Jones came along and chimed right in while attaching her badge to her front pocket. Black couldn't believe it. The couple inside the store he'd just robbed were undercover officers.

"You know what?' whispered Sgt. Mack, "Lets take him down to the station, it's too many witnesses out here."

"Alright Sarg," said Channing, "I'll take him with me and meet you there."

"Uh Uh Uh," Ace was choking from dry mouth after running blocks and blocks.

"Damn baby where you been, look like you just got out of the pool." said Kristi, Ace's longtime girlfriend.

"Naw bae, me and Black just put the police on chase."

"Well where is Black?" Kristi replied.

"He got caught. Remember he got shot, he was running slow and when he tried to jump the gate he fell."

"Why didn't you go back and help him?" she replied.

"The police were too close, they would've gotten me too," he explained.

"Damn baby, what you gon do?"

"Shit, Imma just chill and wait on his call from the county."

"Alright bae, Imma fly down to Western Union to put minutes on the phone. Go and take a shower and be clean when I get back. I'm backed up. You been ducking and dodging me for the last couple of nights," said Kristi.

"Alright girl, hurry back." The door shut as Kristi exited the house.

*Damn, I hope that nigga don't tell the police where I am*, thought Ace. *Naw, he ain't gone tell.*

Jamie Francois

*That's my nigga, and if he do, Imma kill that nigga.*
Those were the thoughts going through Ace's head.

# CHAPTER 2
# BETRAYAL

"Alright James Thompson, aka Black, who was your little friend?" asked Sgt. Mack.

"Man I already told you, I don't know what you're talking bout."

*Waaap!* Sgt. Mack slapped Black in the face again. "You listen here, we've been looking for you and your partner for the last couple of months, you better tell me who he is or you are going to spend the rest of your life in prison."

Black replied, "Man I don't know what you talking bout, plus I ain't do shit to get life in prison."

"Oh, I see you're a rookie to this. Don't you know 1$^{st}$ degree armed robbery carries life if convicted? Not to mention, armed kidnapping," said Sgt Mack.

"Man I ain't kidnap nobody."

"See that's where you're wrong. You and your little homeboy held me and my partner against our own will, which falls under kidnapping. So that's two life sentences. Not to mention you two were dumb enough not to wear a mask, so I'm pretty sure me and my partner wont have a problem identifying you in trial," said Sgt. Mack.

*Fuck! What about Lil James?* thought Black, about his 5-month old son.

"So what's it going to be? You help me and I help you or you do the rest of your life in prison while your friend has fun on the streets not giving a fuck about you," said Sgt. Mack.

*Damn man, I can't snitch on my nigga. That nigga probably would leave me to rot in prison.* Boom! The door slammed as Officer Jones stepped into the interrogation room. "So this is the guy that got my brand new jeans dirty?"

"Yup! That's him," said Sgt. Mack with a smirk on his face. "I just got off the phone with Officer Channing. He is on his way to take him to the county jail," said Jones.

"Naw man wait. His name is Jerrell Pierre," Black had just made the worst mistake ever. He broke the number one street rule. DO NOT SNITCH.

"Okay. Finally, some cooperation. Where does he live?" said Mr. Mack.

*I can't believe I'm doing this, but fuck that. It's either him or me and I ain't doing life in prison,* thought Black. "He lives in Carol City, on 195th and 10th."

"You better not be lying or you're going straight to jail," said Mack. "Chhh…I need a warrant and the SWAT Team here now. We have a location on the second suspect."

"Yeah baby, right there! Keep hitting that spot," yelled Kristi.

"You know I got you baby," responded Ace.

Wap! Wap! went Kristi's fat ass hitting Ace's thighs. Ace was fucking Kristi to death as usual, fast stroking then slowing it down. Ace was slow grinding in Kristi's warm pussy while thick white foam covered Ace's dick.

"I'm cuming baby don't stop!" The sounds of her cries only made Ace go harder.

*BOOM!* The sound of the door hit the ground. "Police! Get the fuck down," one of the SWAT members yelled.

"Yaaaaa," Kristi screamed.

"What the fuck going on?" said Ace.

"You're coming with us," said Officer Mack.

"Who the fuck are you?" Ace asked.

Mack replied, "I'm your worse nightmare. This will be the last day you ever rob anyone again."

"I don't know what the hell you talking about!"

"Yea, yea, yeah. Tell it to the Judge," replied Mack.

"Ok get dressed, time to go", said one of the swat officers. Ace was slowly getting dressed. He couldn't believe what was happening at the time. The officers cuffed him and escorted him out.

[Back at the station]

"So who is James Thompson?" asked Mack.

"I don't know a James Thompson," replied Ace. "Listen, there's no need to lie. Your boy already dropped a dime on you. How do you think we got your address?"

*Fuck. That nigga snitched on me*, thought Ace.

"Plus I can recognize your face from the cellular store."

"Man I ain't rob nobody and I don't know a James Thompson, so ya'll can go ahead and take me to the county," said Ace.

"Ok. Ms. Jones and I will see you in trial," replied Mack and walked out the room.

Ace couldn't believe he was looking at the same person that was in the store that turned out to be an undercover cop. Ace just stared out the window on the way to the county jail. He had had just turned 21 and this isn't how he imagined it would be.

Errr…BOOM! The gate shut behind Ace as he entered the county.

"Ok. Strip naked," said an old fat correction officer.

*Man this place stank as fuck*, thought Ace. After all the procedures were done, Ace was brought to his cell where he would wait to be arraigned in court. All eyes were on him as he entered the cell. *Fuck these niggas looking at*, Ace said to himself.

"Yo Ace what's good?" said Junky Git, a nigga from the hood.

"A, what's good?" he replied.

"Man what you doing here?" Junky Git asked.

"That nigga Black snitched on me, we hit that store up on 183$^{rd}$. I got away, he got caught. Next thing you know they bust in the crib and arrested me."

"Naw man, Black ain't like that."

"How else would they come get me?"

"Damn man you right. That's fucked up. That was your main man." said Junky.

" Fuck that nigga," replied Ace.

"So what you charged with Black?"

"Robbery," he replied.

"Got damn—no bond," he responded while laughing.

"What? No bond? You gotta be playing!" said Black.

"Man I been doing this since a youngin'. Robbery is a PBL (Punishable by Life), which means no bond," said Junky.

*Man I gotta call Kristi*, Ace thought to himself, remembering she put minutes on the phone for Black.


"Hello, baby you alright? It's me Ace. I'm in the county, they took me to jail."

"Imma come bond you out," replied Kristi.

"I don't have a bond—"

"What you mean you don't have a bond?" his girlfriend replied.

"Robbery doesn't come with a bond. I'll be arraigned tomorrow and my first court date will be 21 days from then." Ace had gotten all that information from Junky Git.

"Alright, I'll be there tomorrow. I love you," Kristi said.

"I love you too," replied Ace.


[May 10, 2008]
"Jerrell Pierre," said the judge.

"He's present," said Jerrell's public defender.

"How are you doing your honor."

The judge didn't even give him eye contact. "3 counts of armed robbery with a firearm and two counts of armed kidnapping."

*What the fuck,* thought Ace. *Kidnapping? I ain't kidnap nobody.* This was Aces' first time getting jammed up, so he knew little of the court system.

"NO BOND. Set for trial June 1, 2008!" yelled the judge.

"Psst. come here." Ace called his lawyer.

"Hello, I'm Gordon Murray, here's my card."

"Fuck that. Who said I was going to trial?"

"No, that's not real trial, that's just a date we will come back to check the status of the case," replied Mr. Murray.

"So when am I going home?"

Mr. Murray replied, "See Mr. Pierre, these types of cases aren't really easy, they take time. This isn't the Juvenile Detention Center anymore. This is the big leagues."

"Man just get me home. I ain't do nothing!" yelled Ace.

"Ok. We will be in touch," said Mr. Murray.

*Damn Imma kill that fuck nigga when I see him,* thought Ace. Ace looked in the crowd only to see Kristi in tears. Kristi blew a few kisses and put up a call me sign.

*Fuck. Now I gotta ride in this shit cause that nigga Black. Fuck it. I might as well make this home while I'm here.* Ace was furious. He was going back to the cell and raise hell.

"What happened in court?" asked Junky Git.

"Man them white folks reset me 21 days. It's all good though, now I gotta make the best of this. Look man, I'm fixing to put down on everybody in here, either they break it off or they fight for their shit."

Junky Git replied, "Man this cell ain't like that."

"That lawyer said these cases take a while, so I ain't gone be in here starving and shit," Ace said.

"Starving? All that robbery you do, where yo money at?" asked Git.

See these days the average young nigga was doing either two things: robbing or selling dope. They were doing it for a couple of reasons: to get fresh, buy Jordan's, and trick off with the hoes. See the average nigga never thought about getting caught. So they never put money to the side for lawyers and commissary fees. They blew it just as fast as they got it. "Man you know how that shit is out there. Clubbin, Tricking, getting fresh. Right now I'm fucked up," said Ace.

"All that robbing you do with nothing to show for it. Man fuck that."

"You with me or not?" asked Ace.

"Shit Imma be here for a minute too. You know I'm with you," replied Git. Junky Git was 6 foot 4 inches, 250 pounds. Ace knew he put fear in niggas hearts. See Junky used to box, but he let the streets reel him in. So he would just walk the streets all day clowin. That's how he got his name Junky Git.

"A, Yo Attention in the cell, who is the houseman?" yelled Ace.

"Nigga, I'm the houseman. What you wanna know for?" replied Big Worm.

Ace responded, "Look! From now on. This me and my nigga Git house and all the money in it."

Big Worm said, "You think you gone come on your 2$^{nd}$ day and put down? Nigga I put work in this cell."

"So what you wanna fight for the position?" asked Ace.

"Paint open, lil nigga," said Big Worm. See Big Worm thought it was sweet. He was a little taller than Ace, about 6 foot 2, 220 pounds. Big Worm thought he was just gon go in and whoop up on Ace.

Little did he know he was gone get in the grid with a real heavyweight champion.

"Strap up nigga," said Junky Git.

Big warm eyes opened so big in shock. "What nigga? You want some of this?"

Junky didn't even say a word, he rushed Big Worm like a lion rushing for his prey. BOOM! BOOM! The sounds of the bunks getting crashed into. They were going blow for blow until Ace came out of nowhere with the broom stick. CRACK! Ace hit Big Worm across the head.

"YAAA SHIT" Big Worm yelled. He turned to attack Ace. Too bad, he moved too slow. Junky grabbed him from behind, slammed him, and got on top and took Worm for a ride. Junky beat Big Worm's face in with the lethal blows he had developed from being a boxer.

"Who else want some?" Ace announced. Everybody was looking stupid. The cell was pure coochie just as Ace sensed. "That's what I thought!" he continued.

An officer appeared at the door. "What the hell!" the officer said to himself. "What happened here?"

The whole cell stayed quiet, nobody wanted to say anything, due to the fear they had for Ace and Git. "Chhh, We need a stretcher in cell 3A." Soon two orderlies and a nurse carried Big Worm out the cell.

"Now look. I'm Ace and this Junky," Ace announced to the other inmates. "We got a couple of rules. All the canteen slips will be in my possession, if you ordering—you come to me. Whoever orders, I need 50 percent of everything. I control the TV. Whenever I need the phone, I don't wanna have to wait on it. The showers, I get in before anybody. Ya'll got that?" Everyone nodded in agreement.

"Where you got that broom stick from?" asked Git.

"It was over there in the corner," he replied.

"Man your crazy man, Imma go listen to 99 Jamz."

What you got, a radio?" Ace asked.

"Hell yeah, can't do my time without one," Git replied. Ace looked around to see if he found anyone listening to a radio.

"A Chico, lemme get that radio." Without hesitation, the Chico (JP) brought the radio over the Ace.

"Back that up. What's your name?" asked Ace. He replied to with his name. "Alright. You with us or not?" asked Ace.

"Man I don't want no problems. Ya'll do 'ya'll thing," replied JP.

"That's what I'm talking bout'," Ace whispered to himself.

"What you doing in here?" JP asked.

"My homeboy snitched on me. But Imma soldier. I'll come up out of this." Ace stated.

JP told Ace that he was gonna find a lot of snitches where they were at. "Man it ain't that easy beating charges when you got a co-defendant telling on you," JP said.

"Imma kill that nigga when I get a chance, watch me." Ace said with death written all on his face.

Junky Git yelled out to Ace, "Yo check this out, fuck with me."

Ace replied by expressing his hate for Black again.

"You'll catch him one day, he'll get his, lil bra." replied Git.

BOOM! BOOM! Officer Long was banging on the door and yelled out for count time.

# CHAPTER 3
# GUILTY CONSCIENCE

"Man ya'll crackas let me up out of here. Damn, I told on my dawg. Fuck niggaz in the hood gone ban my ass." Black had still been at the robbery bureau for almost 48 hours.

"Alright, Alright, lets go Mr. Thompson," the correction officer said.

"Finally! Yall had me in that shit for almost two days!" yelled Black.

The officer responded, "Oh well, fuck it. You're a snitch anyway. Don't play stupid. You snitched on your homeboy just to be free. I'm an officer and all, but I still grew up in the streets. I don't condone snitching. Those other officers were talking about the look on your face when they told you that you were gonna get life in prison. They said you told faster than Usain Bolt can run 100 meters."

"Man I don't know what you're talking about," said Black.

Black's guilty conscious was talking to him as he went out the elevator to the stairs. When they got into the black car, the officer's badge read, Mr.

Wilson. "Mr. Wilson why you tripping on me like that. I had to save myself. I got a kid!"

"You knew the consequences before you went out here. You weren't thinking about your kid then, were you?" Mr. Wilson responded.

"Damn right, my baby mama trippin bout clothes and shit, that's why I did what I did. Damn what was I thinking? Now Ace might do some serious time behind me," Black explained.

"That's understandable, but you still don't go ahead and snitch on your homeboy. That's against the G-CODE. You know why I hate snitches so much? See, I grew up in the streets with a single mom. I remember when I was 15 years old and my big brother, Dog Man, was 25 years old. We grew up with no father which left my mom and brother left to take care of me. I loved my big bro."

"Well damn where he at now?" asked Black.

"That's what I'm getting at now if you just be patient," replied Mr. Wilson. He continued, "Well when I was 15 years old, my big bro went with his homeboy to rob a bank. Unfortunately, they go caught. Well his homeboy snitched on him, which landed my brother 25 years in prison. He'll be 50 when he gets out. I'm 30 now, so he's been gone for 15 years. That's what led me to be an officer. I couldn't go down the same path as my brother did. I still see my brother and talk to him all the time."

Ace wondered about the friend who snitched on Mr. Wilson's brother, Mr. Wilson replied, "Lets just say he won't be snitching on anybody anymore. That snitching shit ain't cool man, we as officers only know as much as you guys tell us." Black told Mr. Wilson his stop was up, but before he could leave, Mr. Wilson said, "Ah! Just know one thing, what you did was wrong, now your homeboy might not see the street for a while."

Guilty thoughts rushed through Blacks mind. "Whatever man, I had to lookout for myself, I'm out!" Mr. Wilson's words on Black snitching ways filled his mind.


[March 12]

Black woke from a nightmare where he kept hearing the words of Mr. Wilson repeating, "Snitch ass nigga. What you did was wrong!" His mom was in middle of watching her favorite TV show, The Tyra Banks show when she heard his heavy breathing and asked him if everything was okay. He replied that it was just a nightmare and he would be fine. But something was on Black's mind, so he decided to ask his mother, "I was talking to someone earlier this week and they were explaining a story to me. The story was almost identical to what happened to my brother Pat. The man I met said his brother's name was Dog Man."

His mom stopped and exclaimed, "Oh my God." She could never forget a name like that.

Black continued with his story, "Dog Man went to rob a bank with his homeboy and that dude ended up dying in prison. Dog Man's homeboy got sentenced to 5 years in prison and I remember you told me Pat got 5 years for robbing a bank but after his release he went to the army and died for his country."

Black's mother's eyes swelled with tears. Ms. Thompson couldn't do anything but shake her head up and down. "Ma, have been lying to me about Pat all my life? Why mom, why?"

Ms. Thompson replied, "Baby I couldn't tell you that your brother died in prison. I didn't want you to turn out like your brother. I wanted to show you even though a person makes mistakes, they can still make something out of the situation." Black stood there motionless with no expression.

"We'll talk when I get back," said Ms. Thompson. Black just laid back down. It was killing him inside that he had turned out to be a snitch, just like his big brother.

"Count time! Count time!" yelled Sergeant Long. Everybody stood in place to be counted as the correctional officer walked by them. "38, Officer?" asked Sergeant Long.

"Yeah 38," replied the officer.

"Ok back to what you ladies were doing," stated Sergeant Long.

Ace sat back down on his bunk to think, as Junky Git walked up. "What's good Ace?

"I'm thinking about court that's coming up next week," replied Ace.

"Man just chill. Shit gone work out for you, plus you still young," said Git.

"Man I don't wanna hear that young shit, if it wasn't for Black I wouldn't be in this shit," said Ace.

"Man we chose to live the lives we were living, so we gotta accept the good with the bad, lil bra," explained Git.

"Alright man, we'll see what happens. Imma get on the phone and call Kristi."

"Alright, holla when you done," said Git.

*  *

Ace started walking towards the phone. Another inmate that was using the phone saw Ace coming. He quickly ended his call 5 minutes short to allow Ace to get on the phone.


"Hello baby what's up," said Kristi.

"I'm hanging in there, taking it day by day," replied Ace.

"Baby, you'll be alright. You know Imma ride with you no matter what," said Kristi.

"Yeah baby, I appreciate that, but did you talk to the lawyer yet?" asked Ace.

"Yea, I gotta call back tomorrow, but he didn't sound like he had any good news," said Kristi.

"Puss ass public defenders, they don't do nothing but getting' a nigga a long trip to prison," said Ace.

"Baby, don't talk like that. We gotta have hope!" cried Kristi.

"Yeah you right, Imma hang in there for you. But have you seen that pussy ass nigga Black?" asked Ace.

"No, but I have seen those niggaz yall be around and I exposed his ass. But you know how niggaz is, they probably still gone hang around that nigga," said Kristi.

"*You have one-minute left*," the recorded voice of the operator interrupted them.

"Alright baby, love you. Make sho' you holla at that lawyer," said Ace.

"You know I'm on my job, baby. LOVE YOU," said Kristi.

"LOVE YOU too," replied Ace.

*  *

"What's up. What Kristi talking bout?" asked Junky when Ace got back to his bunk.

"Shit, she just trying to help me keep my head up. She says she seen them boys in the hood and exposed Black," said Ace.

"Yea, them boyz gone ban Black's snitching ass," replied Git.

"I don't care what they do, but I know what Imma do when I get a hold of him," said Ace.

"Every time you talk about Black, I see death in yo' eyes," said Git.

"Yeah nigga cuz that's what it's' gone be," replied Ace.

# CHAPTER 4
# THE LONG RIDE

11 months later

Ace had been riding the county jail for almost a year and had just turned 22. Ace and Git still had the dorm under control the whole time. "Damn man we got all this food I don't got no space for Kristi's letters."

"You get 2 or 3 letters a week," replied Git.

"Nigga stop hatin'," said Ace.

"Hating? Nigga I got hoes. Fuck you talking bout," said Junky Git.

"Ha ha, nigga, I'm fucking wit you," laughed Ace.

"Mail call! Mail call!" screamed the Sergeant Long.

"Washington, Jones, Pierre—"

"Oh shit, that's me," said Ace, before going up to the front to collect his letter.

"Here you go," said Sergeant Long as he handed Ace his mail.

"Ferris Dore," said Ace as he read his name on the envelope. *Man this nigga ain't holla at me in almost a year. Now he wanna write me,"* he thought to himself.

"Damn she ain't even give you a chance to write her back," said Git.

"Naw man, this Fat Boy, from the hood," replied Ace.

"What the fuck he wants? He ain't holla the whole time you've been down," said Git.

"Iunno, but Imma see now," said Ace.

*What's good nigga? Hope you been hanging in there. I know you probably mad at me cause I ain't been in touch, but I had caught a case. I was at Metro West. I saw Kristi at the mall and she laced me up wit what happen. That nigga Black poison. These niggaz out here know what's going on and they still fucking with him. I seen them boyz in the club. I just wanted to let you know I'm here for you no matter what. Whatever you need, holla. This my number 555-555-5555. Love.*

"What he talking bout?" asked Junky Git.

"Shit ...bra keeping it 100. He caught a case and just got out. He say niggaz still fucking wit Black out there," said Ace.

"Hell Naw, I told you, niggaz ain't breed the same no more. Back in the days Black would of been in the dumpster somewhere," replied Git.

"It's all good, them boys will learn their lesson," said Ace.

"Imma go holla at Kristi and see what's up with my case," said Ace.

"Alright, lil bra," replied Git.

* *

"You have a collect call from Ace, to answer, press 1," the recorded operator announced his call.

" Hello baby, what's up," said Kristi.

"Shit what's up, I got a letter from Fat Boy today," said Ace.

"O yea. What he talking bout?"

"Shoot, he told me you told him everything that happen and niggaz from the hood still fucking wit Black,"

"Yeah, I seen them niggaz clownin in the club the other day."

"It's' all good tho. What the lawyer talking bout?" asked Ace. By this stage in the riding process, the public defender had not done anything for Ace. All motions were batted down, and all the pleas were all high.

"Well he said that the prosecutors went down from 20 to 10 years. He also said he don't think that they're gonna go any lower," said Kristi.

"Damn man that fuck ass P.D. Don't do shit for me. Call that puss ass cracker for me," said Ace.

"Hold on, bae," said Kristi. She dialed the public defender before clicking over again.

"Hello. Gordon Murray speaking."

"Hello this is Jerrell Pierre, what's going on wit my case?" asked Ace.

"Well I know you've been locked up for a while, but robberies take time. The good news is they came down from 20 to 10 years."

"Man I ain't taking 10 years," said Ace.

"Well the bad news is the prosecutors plan on taking you to trial if you don't take the plea."

"Well you tell them I said, *let's go*."

"Well I don't think you wanna do that. They have you dead to the wrong. The officers plan on coming to trial to identify you. And you have a Co-Defendant placing you on the scene," said Mr. Murray.

Just then, the recorded operator chimed, "*You have one-minute left.*"

"So think about your situation, cause 9 times out of 10, you're not going to win trial," Murray continued.

"Kristi, man hang up," said Ace.

*Click.* And Mr. Murray was gone.

"Baby you really need to think about what he said. You know Imma be there for you," said Kristi.

"Man, Imma holla at you later, LOVE YOU," said Ace.

"LOVE YOU TOO," replied Kristi.

*   *

"What's good bra, any good news?" asked Git.

"Hell Naw man. Them crackers tryna get me to take 10 years."

"Man listen you got 3 counts of arm robbery and 2 counts of kidnapping, you better take that."

"Man, hell naw."

"Ace you only 22 years old. Tighten up and take it," said Git.

"Damn man. I'll be 31 when I get out."

"No, not really. See, in prison, you get Gain Time. You'll only do 8 years of those 10," explained Git.

Ace just stared into that day, contemplating if he should take the time.

*   *

5 months later

"Jerrell Pierre!" yelled Judge Diaz.

"He's present," said Mr. Murray.

"How are you, Judge Diaz?" asked Ace trying to sound good in front of the judge.

"I'm doing fine, Mr. Pierre. Ok, so do we have a plea?" asked Diaz.

"Yes, your honor," said the prosecutor, Mrs. Caplan. "We are offering a 10-year state prison plea. If not judge, then we are ready for trial."

"Well Mr. Murray, does your client understand his situation?" asked Judge Diaz.

"I'm going to have a talk with him now, your honor." Mr. Murray said, before turning his attention to Ace. They spoke in whispers.

"Man I ain't taking 10 years, you can't talk her down to 7? I'll take 7 right now," Ace hissed.

"Listen, Mr. Pierre, I've been working with Mrs. Caplan for 15 years. She's a bitch. When she says something, she means it. You're not gonna win at trial," said Mr. Murray.

Ace looked over his shoulder into the crowded courtroom to see Kristi with tears in her eyes. Kristi motioned her lips to say, *Take it baby. I got you,* with her thumbs up.

"Alright man, run it," said Ace.

"Your honor, my client is ready to take the plea," said Mr. Murray.

"Ok, Mr. Pierre, please stand up. Are you on any drugs right now?' asked Judge Diaz. Ace stopped and stared at Kristi, "No sir, your honor"

"Ok then, I sentence you to 10 years in the Florida Department of Corrections State Prison," said the Judge.

Ace's heart dropped. 10 years was like a life sentence. Kristi left the courtroom in tears, as the bailiff escorted Ace back to the holding cell.

"Listen kid, I know 10 years might sound long, but those White folks in there had you set up. I heard them saying how they had the boobie trap set up for you. They were gone railroad your ass," said the bailiff. Ace was lost for words; he didn't even respond. "You did the right thing, Young gun. Everything will be alright."

*  *

"What's up bra, anything good happen for you?" Asked Junky Git later that day.

"Hell naw, I took the 10 years," replied Ace.

"Damn, lil bra. I'm sorry to hear that, but they had you dead to wrong," said Git.

"Man, Imma take a nap," said Ace, weary with the weight of his predicament.

"Alright man, stay focused," replied Git.

"Hello baby, what's up? Are you alright?" asked Kristi.

"Yea, I'm good, just maintainin'. I need you to call Fat Boy for me. Tell him I need some money put on my canteen, so I'll already have money when I go up the road," said Ace. Now that he'd been sentenced, they would be sending him to a prison camp.

"Alright bae, I got you. You know Imma stick it out wit you, right?"

"Man, I got 10 years. If that pussy itch, you gone scratch it," said Ace.

"Nigga, don't try me like that! We've been together too long for me to let one of these lame ass niggas fuck us up!" yelled Kristi.

"Man, Imma holla at you. You getting' on my nerves."

"Whatever nigga. You trippin'. BYE!" Kristi just hung up in his face. Ace was going through it since he got sentenced. He'd been stressing.

*  *

Kristi was shopping at the grocery store when Ms. Thompson spotted her.

"Hey Kristi, how are you?" said Ms. Thompson.

Kristi gave her the stank face. "Um I'm not doing good ever since your son got my man 10 years in prison," she replied bitterly.

"What are you talking bout?" asked Ms. Thompson, genuinely perplexed. She always had a good relationship with Kristi.

"You know what I'm talking 'bout. Black snitched on Ace about a robbery they did, and now, Ace has to go to prison for 10 years!" Kristi cried.

*O my God, he turned out just like his brother*, thought Ms. Thompson.

* *

"Daddy! Daddy!" screamed Lil Black.

"What's up, Baby Boy?" Black spoiled his son. He gave him whatever he wanted. It was 2:30 in the afternoon and Lil Black was pointing to the cereal box on top of the refrigerator.

"Alright, alright, I'll fix you a bowl," said Black.

Just then, the front door slammed. *Boom*! .

*What the hell!* thought Black. He had the feeling it was one of Ace's homeboys coming to kill him.

"Baby we need to talk." Ms. Thompson appeared in the kitchen doorway.

"Mom! You scared the shit out of me!" screamed Black.

"Sit down. We need to have a talk."

"Mom, if it's about Pat—"

"Boy, if you don't sit down. It's' about you," said Ms. Thompson.

Black stared in his mother's eyes and knew there was something wrong. She was breathing heavy and had a crazy look in her eyes.

"I just ran into Kristi and she told me something about Ace catching 10 years because of you."

Black's heart almost jumped out of his chest. *Damn, bra caught 10 years?* thought Black. "Mom, I don't know what you're talking 'bout," he said.

Waaap! Ms. Thompson slapped Black across the face so hard and fast he didn't even see it coming. "Boy don't you lie to me. Kristi wouldn't just make up nothing like that. She said you told on Ace after getting caught in a robbery."

"Man she lying!" yelled Black.

"That's why I haven't been seeing Ace, and *you* told me he was out of town somewhere," said Ms. Thompson.

Black had too much pride to admit to her that he turned out just like his brother. "Look mom, I don't know what she's talking bout, she's lying."

"You know what? Get out!"

"*What?* Get out?"

"Yea. Get. Out. I'm your mother, I've been raising you for 21 years. I can see that you're lying all over your face."

"Alright, I'm out, I'll be back for my stuff and Lil Black later." Black walked out, slamming the front behind him.

# CHAPTER 5
# SHIT GETS REAL

"Ace, what's good? The bus should be coming to get you any day now," said Junky Git.

"You ain't gotta remind me, man," said Ace.

"Man quit stressin'. You gone be alright. You got a good girl. You got your family. Man, you good," said Git.

"Yea. We'll see, But I gottta go up this road and start working out," said Ace.

"Yeah man, you gottta put on a little weight. So if something ever happens, you can protect yourself," explained Git.

"Wherever I land, Imma take over. Watch me."

"Man, prison ain't sweet like this county jail. People die up that road for shit we pulling in here," explained Git.

"I'll be alright, I got a finesse game. See, I learned muscling shit ain't always good," said Ace.

"Alright now, go up the road and stay focused. Work out get your gain time in, so you can make it out early. You already got almost two years in. Just go and chill so you can make it back in one piece," explained Junky Git.

"Yeah man. I got you, quit crying," said Ace.

"Nigga come here."

"Alright, Alright!" yelled Ace. Junky Git playfully put Ace in a headlock, trying to keep his mind off prison.

*   *

"I would like to deposit this money in this person's account please," said Fat Boy. There was a fine redbone at the counter. Fat Boy thought to himself, *Man, I gotta have her*.

"ID please," asked the teller.

"Here you go," Fat Boy handed her his ID.

"So, Ferris, can I have umm...Jerrell Pierre's D.C. Number?" asked the teller.

" Yea, it's M72425," said Fat Boy.

"How much are you trying to deposit?" asked the teller.

Fat Boy pulled out five hundred dollar bills. "All this," answered Fat Boy.

"Wow. You ballin', huh?"

" Naw, I just do my thang a lil piece, nothing major."

"Ok, well, all done. He should have the money within the next 24 hours," said the teller.

"Ok, thank you, but I also wanna know can I take you out tonight?" he asked her.

"Uh no, Luther Vandross. But you can have my number so we can get to know each other first," she replied.

"That's cool."

She handed him a receipt with her number on it. Fat Boy smiled and exited the store.

*   *

Black was walking down in the hood when he spotted Spook and Puggy....

"What's good yall boys," asked Black.

"Shit, just chilling," answered Spook and Puggy, two dudes from the hood. They heard about Black snitching, but didn't quite believe it.

"Man, I gotta get some money. My ole girl just kicked me out," said Black.

"Damn man that's fucked up. What she kicked you out for?" asked Spook.

"Bullshit, we got into an argument," said Black.

"Well listen, you be on that robbin' shit and we been plotting on this Brinks truck for about a month now," said Spook.

Black quickly thought about it. His first encounter with the law did not go smoothly, but he thought, *Fuck it. I gotta get a place for me and Lil Black.*

"Hold on, hold on. Listen Black, no disrespect, but word around the hood is you that you snitched on Ace for a robbery yall did, and now he gotta do 10 years," said Puggy.

"Man, hell naw. I don't know where yall heard that from. Ace got fucked up on his own," replied Black.

"Man listen, we don't know who to believe. But if you know you snitchin', just don't even get involved in this lick," said Puggy.

"Nigga, I just *told* you. That shit ain't true!" yelled Black.

"Man, yall two niggas chill. Listen Black, the shit going down in two weeks and this is the plan…

*　*

1 week later.

*Tap, Tap, Tap.* The officer was hitting Ace's bunk with his pen.

"Man, what's up," said Ace barely awake.

"Pierre, pack it up, you're out of here."

Ace drowned his face in the pillow, trying to prepare himself mentally for the experience he was about to endure.

"Wake up nigga," said Ace, as he pushed Git to wake him.

"What's up man."

"I'm gone bra."

"Yeah, you leaving?"

"Yeah, they just woke me up. I'm out of here," said Ace.

"Damn lil bra, Imma miss you," said Git.

"Nigga, get off that emotional shit. I don't have a life sentence," said Ace."

"Still nigga, you know I fuck wit you," said Git.

"Man you already know what it is. We gone see each other again," said Ace.

"Pierre, tighten up, it's time to go. Kiss all your girlfriends goodbye!" yelled the officer.

"Alright bra, I'm out."

"Yeah man, remember what I said. Go up there and chill," said Git.

"Alright Bra, LOVE," said Ace.

"Love," Git repeated.

Fifteen minutes later, Ace was on the bus heading to South Florida's reception center. *Damn Black, you got me fucked up in this shit*, he thought. *It's all good though. I'm a soldier, I'll come out on top*, he thought as he dozed off to sleep.

*  *

"Alright you little bitches, welcome to South Florida's reception center," said the officer. Ace jumped out of his sleep.

"What the fuck going on," said Ace.

"My name is Sergeant Bennet, and I am your daddy for today. I better not hear any talking. You're gonna get off this bus, then we're gonna search all your property, you're gonna strip naked for a body search, cut your head bald, see a medical and last, but not least, you're gonna get your blues and hygiene. We have two hours to get this complete," yelled Sergeant. Bennett.

*This gone be a long day*, Ace thought to himself.

"Ok now you lil fuckers, get off my bus!" yelled the Sergeant.

Soon they were inside, in a group circle, fully naked. "Ok, everybody run your fingers through your hair...now rub your finger between your lips...ok, now lift your nuts. Drop them and spread your ass cheeks, bend over, squat and cough." *Cou cou*, came the sounds of about 28 inmates coughing at once. *Man this shit gay as fuck*, thought Ace.

"Ok. Now these 4 inmates are going to handle the rest. You're going to see medical and do everything else I said!" shouted Sgt. Bennett.

All Ace could think about was killing Black for putting him through this experience. He though of shooting him in the face, then stabbing him repeatedly and throwing him off a building. *Man, this is gonna be a long ride*, he thought.

"Next man for a hair cut!" yelled the inmate.

Ace stood up and sat in the chair. "Aye bra, don't go against the grain on my shit," said Ace. In the county jail everybody spent their time brushing their hair. Ace was dogging pretty nice.

"Listen bra, I ain't the police. I'm just doing my job. I see you doing your thang, so Ima give you a 1, but you gotta duck and dodge Sergeant," said the inmate.

"Alright, bet," Ace replied.

# Chapter 6
# It's Going Down

2 WEEKS LATER.

"Man where the fuck is the truck?" asked Puggy.

"It should be here any minute," replied Spook.

"You said that 5 minutes ago," said Puggy.

"Man yall chill and stay focused," said Black. Black was in the back seat, shaking inside. He just wanted this lick to go down smoothly. Spook, Puggy and Black all had fully loaded AK-47s. They were parked outside of Home Depot early in the morning waiting to strike.

"It's 6:05am, he was supposed to be here 5 minutes ago," Puggy went on.

"Shut up. There's the truck pulling in now," said Spook.

*Click clack,* went the AKs being cocked back.

"Let's do this," said Puggy, as the Brinks truck pulled up to the Home Depot. An old white man jumped out the truck with an empty bag.

"Ok, he in the store," said Puggy. "Now let's go wait on the other side of the truck. You ready Black?"

Black was in the back seat nervous as fuck. He had a bad feeling about this lick, but he was already locked in. "Yeah I'm good. Let's ride."

They exited the all black Crown Victoria, all dressed in SWAT gear from the helmet to the boots. "Ok, he coming now," said Spook.

"Black, remember, make sure he stays down on the ground before you run back to the car," said Puggy.

"Alright," replied Black.

As soon as the driver hit the corner of the truck, Puggy already had the butt of the assault rifle turned around and drove it straight into the man's stomach. "OHHHH!" the driver moaned in pain. He fell straight to the floor, and curled up like a little baby. Spook picked up the big bag of money and ran to the car. Black held the man at gunpoint while he lay on the ground.

"I got this Puggy. Go meet with Spook and come get me," said Black.

"Alright," Puggy replied.

Puggy ran towards the car. Black stood there nervous, looking around for the security guard that usually circles the plaza.

"O shit!" Black just saw the guard's car coming down the street towards him and the truck.

"CHH...this is Mr. Watson. I think I have a robbery in progress. I'm going to need backup immediately." The guard spotted the situation and called it in.

"10-4," said another security officer inside the building.

*Where the fuck they at?* thought Black.

*Errrrr*, the Crown Vic came up along side him. "Get in Black. Tighten up," said Spook.

The whole time, the Brinks driver was laying on the side where his gun was in the holster. He was clutching his 357, waiting for Black to slip. Black opened the back door and dove in the backseat. The driver got up quickly and fired a shot straight through the passenger seat striking Puggy in the temple. Blood splattered everywhere.

"O shit! Go Spook, take off!" yelled Black.

Errrrr, the Crown Vic sped away. "What the *fuck* Black? You ain't grab the nigga gun like you was supposed to? asked Spook.

"Man I ain't see no gun!" replied Black.

"Nigga that was your role in this *whole plan*! While you got him down on the ground, check his waist for any weapons!" yelled Spook. Black looked at the halfway cut off head leaning over towards Spook and he vomited all over the backseat.

Spook was trying to get away, but the security vehicle was on his tail. "Fuck I can't lose this fuck ass security guard!" yelled Spook. He busted a right, only to run head on with a Miami-Dade police squad car. Black hit his head in the back of the driver's side and Spook was knocked out immediately. Black opened the door trying to run, but stumbled and fell. When he regained consciousness he had a Dade-County officer on his ass.

"Get the fuck down!" the officer screamed. *Chhhh*, he spoke into the walkie talkie on his shoulder with one hand, while the other hand held his gun pointed at black. "This is officer Johnson. I have both suspects in custody. We are going to need paramedics we have one dead in the car."

"We have paramedics on the way," said officer Kelly. There were squad cars everywhere. A news truck arrived and soon the street was filled with news reporters trying to get a glimpse of the action.

Black woke up in the squad car only to see officer Kelly staring him right at him from the passenger seat. "Well, well, well, James Thompson. You just didn't learn your lesson, did you?" Black dropped his head. "Ok, lets head to the station, Johnson," Kelly said.

As the car drove away, Black watched in horror as they were taking Puggy's body out of the car. At the station, Black still couldn't believe what happened. He passed an interrogation room and saw Spook with his head down on the table.

"Ok, sit tight. Officer Kelly will be here to talk to you soon," Johnson said.

Black's mind was racing. Would he be the one charged with murder? Officer Kelly entered the room with a serious look on her face. "There's not much to say. You're being charged with armed robbery and murder."

"Murder? Man I ain't kill nobody!"

"Yea, but someone got killed in the act of a crime you were involved in."

"I don't know what you talking 'bout,"

"Ok, we will see, Mr. Thompson. See you in court."

*Damn man, what the fuck was I thinking? These crackers finna bam my ass*, thought Black.

*   *

"Haaaa!" The crowd was going crazy on the rec field at the basketball court.

"That's my nigga!" yelled Ace.

"Yea, he's pretty good," said Trouble.

"Man he was supposed to go to the NBA,"

"Naw man, he ain't that good."

"You crazy! He ballin' on these niggaz."

"Yea, this prison though. These niggaz ain't that good."

Ace landed in one of the sweetest camps in Florida. He was being housed at Belle Glades C.I. There was weed, coke, heroin, crack, and cell phones. Whatever you wanted, Belle Glades had it.

"Man all this money floating around, we gotta find a connect," said Trouble.

"What's good, yall boyz," said Tron.

"We chillin, I see you on that court, boy. You killin these niggaz," said Ace.

"Ye appreciate that bra."

*Brrrrr! "Rec yard is over. Please report to your assigned dormitories."*

"Alright yall boyz. Imma holla," said Ace. They all gave each oher dap and went to their rooms.

# CHAPTER 7
# A LONG ROAD AHEAD

"James Thompson," said the Judge.

"He's present, Judge Rodriguez," said Mr. Williams. He was one of the best attorneys in Dade County. Black's mom put up her house just to pay for him.

"Do we have a plea on the table?"

"Yes we do your honor. We are offering Mr. Thompson 40 years state prison, with 25 years minimum mandatory."

"Uh, your honor, can I please have a moment with my client?"

"Yes, you may."

The bailiff uncuffed Black and took them to a small room.

"Man, I'm not taking 40 years!" Black screamed.

"Listen I know it's a hard pill to swallow, but you're dead wrong,"

"Man what the fuck my mom paying you all this money for if I gotta take 40 years?"

"We can go to trial, but you were caught at the scene, red handed with a dead body,"

"I ain't kill nobody."

"Yea, but he was killed in the act of a crime *you* committed. It's Florida Law."

Tears welled up in Blacks' eyes at the thought of not seeing Lil Black for 40 years.

"I mean, it's your decision. You have to remember at the end of the day, I go home regardless. You have to think of your family at this point."

"Can you reset this court date, so I can get my mind together?"

"Ok, I'll try, but we don't want to get this prosecutor pissed off. We're lucky we even got a plea bargain."

Black's head dropped in disappointment.

* *

"We have a fight in the chow hall. We need backup!" yelled an officer on the radio.

"Damn that shit was crazy," said Ace.

"Yeah man those gangs stay going threw it," replied Trouble.

"I ain't gone lie. I like the way those DSG boyz move."

"Please don't tell me you plan on getting into a gang."

"They not a gang. They only call they self Down South Gangsters. It's just everybody from Dade, Broward, and Palm Beach sticking together."

"Man, it's the same shit."

"Everybody back to your dorms!" yelled an officer.

"I ain't even finish *eating*," said Ace.

"Yea, well welcome to the chain game," replied Trouble, getting up from the table. "I'll holla at you bra, LOVE."

"Alright, LOVE," replied Ace.

* *

2 WEEKS LATER

"Man yall stuck. Yall went seven books. That's 6 all day where I'm from," said Ace. Ace was real good in Spades. He spent most of his time either playing cards or working out. "That's ten dollars, pay up time!"

"Aye bra, let me holla at you." Ace looked up to see a dude from Broward asking to speak to him.

"Aye put that money on my bunk. Anyway what's good Tim?"

"What's up Ace, check it out. Me and my brothers been watching you and we wanna fuck wit you."

"What you mean, Tim?"

"Well we wanna bring you home as one of our brothers."

"Shit….man, Iunno. I'm just chillin right now. I'm tryna get this gain time to make it home."

"Man these niggaz fear us, you don't gotta worry about gettin in trouble too much. It's just about LOVE, loyalty, and respect. We getting money man, fuck wit us."

"Imma see Tim. When I make up my mind, I'll holla at you."

"Alright man, fuck wit me."

*　*

## 1 YEAR LATER -2010-NOV

It was rough enough for Black this past year. Every cell he went to he got beat. Everybody got a whiff that Black was a snitch. These niggas gave Black so much hell that he had to be placed under PM (Protective Management). His baby momma was shitting on him and his mom damn near gave up on him.

"Your honor we are here to accept the 30 year state prison term."

"Does your client understand that the 30 years will be mandatory?"

"Yes, he does, your honor."

"Mr. Thompson let me explain something to you. You are very lucky to come out this good. The state did not have to offer you a plea."

"Yes, your honor."

"Ok well, Mr. Thompson, may you please stand."

Black's mom was in the crowd with Lil Black. Lil Black was two and a half and growing quickly, but he was too young to understand what was happening. Ms. Thompson just stared at Black, crying her eyes out.

"Did anybody force you to take this plea?"

"No sir."

"Are you on any drugs?"

"No sir."

"Ok, I sentence you to 30 years mandatory state prison."

Blacks' mind went blank at the thought of spending the rest of his life in prison.

"What about the co-defendant?" asked Judge Rodriguez.

"He's in the back right now, we have an 8 year plea deal for him."

*What the fuck? Eight years?* Thought Black.

"Ok Mr. Thompson time to go," said the bailiff.

As Black passed the holding cell he ran into Spook. Spook looked up at Black and smiled.

"What goes around comes around," said Spook. Black was so shocked; he didn't know what to say.

# CHAPTER 8
# LET'S GET MONEY

"Inmate Pierre, head down to the Captain's office!" yelled the correctional officer.

"O shit," said Tron. "That might be a piss test, you better go drink that water."

Ace ran to the sink with a cup and drank five big cups of water.

"Ok, now piss one time," said Tron. "Then drink one more cup and you should be good."

"Alright bra. Imma let you know what happens."

* *

"Listen, Lieutenant Brown, we need the compound secured at a certain time in order to bring the truck in and out," said Carter. Carter was an old school dude from the hood. He started as an officer and made his way up to warden, the boss of the whole compound.

"Ok, Mr. Carter, the pride building should take one more week to be cleaned out completely."

"Well we're gonna be rich. I got 100 bricks coming in every Monday night."

*What the fuck! 100 bricks?* Thought Ace as he listened outside the door.

"Well you can't just bring any truck in here."

"Yeah I know. That's why I got a little something going on with the canteen company to use one of their trucks."

"Wow good one, the inmates will never suspect anything."

"Ok Lieutenant. We'll talk some more business later."

As the lieutenant walked out, Ace got into position as if he was never listening. "How long have you been out here?"

"Not long," replied Ace. Lieutenant Brown just stared at him and walked away.

"I'm here to see the captain."

"Well you have the wrong office, said Carter. The captain is the last door down the hall and to the right."

"Ok."

"Hey listen, how long were you out there?"

Ace paused "Not too long."

"Yeah whatever. How much did you hear?"

"Mr. uh…" (Ace paused as he looked at the name tag) "Carter. I ain't no snitch I heard what's going on, but that ain't got nothing to do with me."

"Haha, you ain't no snitch huh? I heard that plenty of times, but to make sure, how much do you love money?"

"Man I *love* money!"

"Ok, well I'm gonna drop a few ounces in your hand. You can sell 50 and 100 pieces, or maybe even the whole ounce."

"Ok so, when do I re-up?"

"Well that depends on you. The faster you move it, the faster you re-up."

"Alright, Mr. Carter. I got you. When do I start?"

Carter opened the drawer and then threw 4 nicely compressed ounces at Ace. "You can start now."

*Damn, WTF!* Thought Ace.

"Listen, what gang are you in?"

"I'm not in a gang."

"Well you better get with somebody, cause once these niggas get a whiff that your the dopeman, they gone be trying you."

"Well, I think I got some niggas in mind."

"Ok, well get money uh….inmate Pierre."

"Alright Mr. Carter."

"A, and don't worry about the captain. It's probably a piss test. I'll cover for you."

"Shit, bet. I'll see you later."

Ace walked out the office with nothing but money on his mind. *It's time to get rich in the chain game. DSG here I come*, thought Ace.

*  *

2 WEEKS LATER

Black was in prison in no time. He knew it was gonna be rough for him, especially if he ran into any of those dudes from the county jail.

"How are you doing, Mr. Thompson?" said Ms. Etter. Ms. Etter was Black's classification officer.

"I'm alright."

"Ok well here's your release date."

"June 4th, 2039," thought Black as he read the date. "I can't get out no earlier than this?

"Well no. You have a 30 year mandatory sentence."

*My life is over*, thought Black.

"Would you like to get into school or take up any vocational trades?"

"Yeah, I would like to take my G.E.D. and attend courses for my CDL license. I hear they have a good program at Belle Glades C.I."

"Ok, well I'm not making any promises, but I will sign you up."

"Ok, thank you."

* *

"A Tim, check it out." Ace spotted Tim walking around the rec field

"What's good Ace?"

"I was thinking about taking you up on that offer."

"Ok, so you wanna fuck with us?"

"Yeah and I got something to bring to the table."

"Oh yeah? And what's that?"

"Ok well…"

* *

Unfortunately, Black didn't make it to Belle Glades as he expected. Instead, he got shipped to a camp called Ham C.I.

*Damn that was a long ride*, thought Black. After going through all the in-take procedures, Black and the rest of the new inmates were escorted to their cells. Black walked in the dorm to see niggas everywhere.

"What's up? Where you from," Black's new bunky asked.

"I'm from Dade County."

"Oh yeah, I heard yall got some good cocaine down there."

"Yeah, it's alright."

"Well welcome to Horrible Ham."

"So that's what they call this place?"

"Yeah, it's fucked up in here.

"Where you from?"

"I'm from St. Petersburg."

"Where's that at?"

"You don't know where St. Pete's at?"

"No, I'm from Dade County, that's all I know."

"It's in Pinellas County, closer to Clearwater.

"Ok, well what's up with this dorm?"

"It's alright, but it can get a little out of hand sometimes."

"What usually happens?"

"Well, if it's not gangs going through it, it's about money. Usually gambling."

"What about the officers?"

"You got some good ones. But, for the most part, they're all assholes."

"Chowtime, class A uniform!" yelled the dorm officer.

"Class A? What's that," asked Black.

"Blue shirt, pants, I.D.,"

"Ok, what we got for lunch?"

"Most likely bullshit."

While the dorm walked to chow, Black was looking around, hoping not to run into anybody from the county. He didn't want to have the name Snitch in prison. As they entered the chow hall, Black grabbed his tray. " *What the fuck is this?* Thought Black, looking at the food.


"Oh shit, look who just got here," said Spook.

"Who?" replied Junky Git.

"That snitching ass nigga Black! He right there grabbing his tray."

"Man that nigga got my dawg 10 up the road; I'm finna flip that nigga," said Git.

"How you gone don that?"

"When they call rec,  slide in his dorm and fire his ass up."

"Alright look, Imma meet you halfway and make sure you get out safe."

* *

Back at his dorm, Junky Git was getting ready to handle business. He took a belt and tied it up to a throw away lock. He was gonna bash Black's head in.

"Get ready for recreation!" yelled the dorm officer.

*Show time*, thought Git.

* *

"What's up what took you so long?" asked Spook when he got back to the chow hall.

"I had to get the shit ready."

"Ok well, I just had that Chico JP you was wit in the county go in there to see what he doing. He said he sleep."

"Ok, easier for me."

Junky Git crept into the dorm and looked around for Black. Once he spotted him, he took the belt with the lock attached to it out of his pants and made his way towards Black's bunk. *This one's for you, Ace*, thought Junky Git as he cocked his arm so far back and hit Black right in the face with the lock.

"Yaaa!!!" yelled Black.

Blood was everywhere. Junky Git ran towards the door before Black could get a glimpse of him.

"Yaaaaa!!!" Black continued to yell. The dorm officer looked to see what all the yelling was about only to find Black walking towards the officer station holding his face full of blood. *Chhh.* "We have an inmate bleeding and we need medical to Golf dorm as soon as possible."

Black fell to the ground, he was seriously injured.

# CHAPTER 9
# BACK TO THE MONEY

3 WEEKS LATER

Ace and his DSG Boyz were getting money in no time. They had the compound on smash. By now Ace had a nice chunk of money saved up with Kristi.

"Baby, what's up?" asked Ace.

"I'm alright, I went and got that money."

"Oh yeah? That's good. Where we at now?"

"Eight grand."

"Damn, already?"

"Yeah bae, it's been coming in fast."

"Shit. At the rate I'm going, we should be straight in 5 more years when I get out."

"Yeah, don't get too comfortable. You know good things don't last forever."

"Alright baby. You coming this weekend?"

"Yeah, I'll be there."

"Ok make sure you bring that white girl, Keisha, with you."

"Ok I'll see if she wanna come with me."

"Alright bae, love you."

"Love you too."

It had only been about a month and a half and Ace was booming. He was really going to take off now that he had convinced Kristi to bring in cocaine and some new drug called K-2.

"What's good Tim?"

"Chillin man, bout to make something to eat."

"Yeah I see you doing your thing. You got bout 4-5 lockers in this bitch,"

"Yeah thanks to you."

"What about the other brothers? Did everybody get money on their card?"

"Yeah everybody straight."

"Ok, but did you order their shoes and winter clothes? You know we can't walk around here looking like shit eaters."

"Yeah man, all that is taken care of. Don't worry bout nothing."

"Alright bra, Imma slide down to the warden's office to re-up. We gone package everything tonight."

"Alright holla."

* *

" How you doing Mr. Carter?"

"I'm doing just fine, and you?"

"Shit, I wish I wasn't in this shit, but other than that, it couldn't be better."

"Well that's good to hear. How can I help you?"

"I'm ready for another package, sir."

"God damn! This is your 6th time this month. We must have some junkies on the compound."

"I guess people like to get high," Ace shrugged his shoulders.

"Wow, you making more than the average trap house on the street."

"Yeah, I'm doing my thing a lil."

"Ok, well here."

Warden Carter tossed Ace ten small compressed ounces. Ace went on to pack them in his socks and waistline.

"Let's see how fast you get rid of those."

"No pressure, watch me."

"I appreciate you keeping the compound under control while I do my thang," Carter said.

"Your welcome. You know the old saying. One hand washes the other."

"Yeah well, as long as we're both happy."

"I'll see you later, Mr. Carter. "

"Ok yeah, the truck will be comin' in kind of late today. So don't be surprised."

"Alright."

* *

Black was laying in confinement staring at the ceiling thinking about everything in the past. Thinking about Lil Black, his big brother Pat, both robbery situations... *I wonder what's going on with Ace*, he thought. Black was seriously injured. He had to get surgery for his face and it was taking a while to heal.

"So Bunky, you don't know who hit you with the lock?"

"For the 100th time, I told you I don't know. It was my first day at the camp."

"Damn he got you pretty good whoever it was."

"Yeah, don't remind me."

"At least you get a free transfer from this hell hole."

"Alright man, I'm gone to sleep. I got too much on my mind."

* *

LATER THAT NIGHT 1AM

Ace and Tim was breaking down the weed and preparing packages for all the brothers.

"Shit, this the most we ever had at one time, " said Ace proudly.

"Yeah that means mo' money mo problems," Tim said.

"Man these niggaz ain't crazy. They see we ain't had a problem yet."

*Beep. Beep. Beep.* Outside, the truck was backing up into the pride building.

"Damn the truck here kinda late today," said Tim, looking out the window.

"Yeah Mr. Carter told me it was gonna be late."

"Damn man Mr. Carter getting money."

"Yeah, him *and* Lieutenant Brown," said Ace and joined Tim to stare out the window.

"They gotta be fucking with at least 200 bricks or better."

"I don't know, but they better not get caught or they ass gone be right here with us," said Ace.

"There goes your baby, Sergeant Lewis."

"Man, Imma go see if I can get the pussy. Watch out for me." Ace took off in hot pursuit.

"What's up Sergeant, you working here tonight?"

"Naw. I'm just letting your dorm officer get her hour break." Sergeant Lewis was something to die for, especially in her uniform. She wore shorts above her knees, with her boots and that ass would turn heads no matter where she stepped on the compound.

"Sergeant, why you been playing with me? You know I want you."

"Boy, like I said, you get that money up and maybe we can talk."

"Money ain't nothing, man. I got money."

"Yeah, I heard that plenty of times."

"You better go check my account. I'm not just rapping."

"Ok. We'll see. In the meantime, here, take this. There's a number already logged in there. When you're ready to send some money, that person will tell you where to send it and then we'll see what we can do."

"Alright Sergeant. You know Imma beat it up. Right?"

"Boy, please. We will see."

*  *

"Damn she still acting stank with the pussy?"

"Yeah, but she talking money."

"Shit, money ain't no thang."

"Yeah. That's what I told her, and she gave me this." Ace pulled out the cell phone Sergeant gave him.

"Yeah. You good. You got her right where you want her."

"Yeah well, now I can finally make moves with this."

"Shit. Finally I can run down on my baby momma. You know she shitting on me."

"Man you know how them hoes is. Out of sight out of mind."

* *

2 MONTHS LATER, APRIL 2011

"Mr. Thompson pack it up. You're out of here," said the officer.

"Finally, God *damn*! Yall had me in here for two months and some change."

"Yeah well, I'm not classification. I'm just an officer."

"You know where I'm going?"

"Well, yeah, but I can't tell you. It's' a security risk."

"Ok well get me out of this shit."

* *

"Hey baby," said Kristi. Kristi had been to visitation almost every week. Once she got used to bringing in that package, the sky was the limit for her and Ace.

"What's good, bae." Their lips locked in a long passionate kiss.

"Lets' sit down. You got that?"

"Yeah I got it, all packaged how you want it."

"Ok, see that punk over there? When we go take pictures you gone pass it off to him."

"And what he gone do with it?"

"He gone stick it up his ass."

"What the hell? Up his *ass*? And you gone touch it?"

"Listen, just do what I say. Let me handle this."

"Whatever boy. Anyway that phone sex last night was good. I nutted twice."

"Yeah well, you know yo nigga got that type of effect."

"Uh huh. I can't wait for you to be inside of me again."

"And I've been working out, so you know this back strong. I got something for that pussy."

"I love you."

"I love you too."

The punk gave Ace a signal as he walked to the bathroom to get everything ready. When the punk came out, Ace and Kristi were already in line waiting. Kristi walked over and handed the punk the package.

"Alright bae, you gone be here next week?"

"I'll see, if you behave this week."

"Yeah whatever.  See you next week. Love you."

Ace left the visiting part and went straight to the rec yard to workout.

"Damn boy I see you getting big," said Troub.

"Yeah man, you know I'm getting short."

"Yeah man, you gained a lot of weight."

Since Ace came to prison he'd been working out. He came in 149lbs and was now 190lbs solid.

"You tryna get out there to that baby big and healthy."

"Ha ha ha," Ace and Troub shared a laugh.

"What's up with Tron?"

"He on the court."

"Yall been gettin that package?"

"Hell yeah, back that up."

"I got like 6000 on my card."

"Damn nigga how the hell?"

"Shit, I haven't been smoking like that. Straight mail outs. Fuck that dime and dub shit."

"Boy I like that. You showing me discipline and you real business minded."

"Man, these niggaz love that K-2 shit."

K-2 was a new drug going around. Really it was incense or spice, but it got you instantly high and didn't show up in your piss. So it was a hot commodity in prison.

"Yeah man, it don't show up when they piss test a nigga, so you know these niggaz love that shit."

"Tron what's up," asked Ace.

"Chillin man just maintaining."

"Boy you putting on weight Tron."

"Yeah thanks to you, that K-2 is the best thing that happened to this compound. I been eating good, my card is flooded."

"That's what I like to hear, yall boyz just keep it up.".

# CHAPTER 10
# LET THE GAMES BEGIN

Welcome to Belle Glades C.I. the sign read.

*Belleglades*, thought Black. *This is the camp I was originally supposed to go to!*

After all the correct procedures, Black and the rest of the inmates were escorted to their dorms.

"All new gains, please report to the officer station," said the dorm officer.

Black and the rest of the inmates reported to the officer booth.

"I'm officer Warren and I'll be your daytime dorm officer. Wow, what happened to your face?" asked Officer Warren, looking at Black. It was still swollen and had a bruise on it.

"I got into a little altercation at my last camp."

"Ok, well you better not bring that bullshit to my dorm, understood?"

"Yes ma'am."

"Anyway, I have 3 rules, very simple. Keep the noise down, keep your pants up and keep your dick in your pants."

Everyone nodded in agreement and walked away.

"What's good foo? Where you from?" asked Black's new bunky L.G.

"I'm from Carol City."

"Hell yeah, well you got a lot of home team here."

"Yeah…like who?" asked Black.

"Uh you got a lot from Dade County, but the only one I remember from Carol City is Ace."

Black's eyes widened so far apart you would think his eyeballs were about to fall out.

"Ace? How does he look?"

"A brown skin nigga, he about 23 or 24, kinda big 'bout 188 pounds."

Everything sounded about accurate except the weight. Black didn't remember Ace to be so big.

* *

"Mail Call!" yelled Ace's dorm officer. "Pierre!"

"Aye yo, Ace, Ace," yelled Tim as he shook Ace out of his sleep.

"What's up?"

"You got mail."

Ace got up to get his letter. The front of the envelope read Kristi Pierre.

*Man, I just wrote this girl*, thought Ace. When Ace opened the letter it wasn't Kristi's handwriting.

*What's good Ace, it's Junky Git. Yeah man, dem crackers got me with the 15 piece. It's all good though. I had one of your letters in my property, that's how I got Kristi's address. I got some good news. I ran into that nigga Black. He up the road too. I don't know for what or how much time, but he landed where I'm at now and I flammed his ass up. I got him from round here ASAP. You already know, lil bra, it's love so I had to handle up for you. Remember stay out of trouble. LOVE!*

"Ace couldn't believe what he was reading. He was surprised, confused, but happy.

"What's good Ace, that's that baby, huh?"

"Naw that's my homeboy from the hood. He was just letting me know he handled some business for me."

"Oh ok, shit that's straight."

"Yeah my puss ass co-d snitching on me. My dawg ran into him and fired his ass up."

"Damn that's a real homeboy."

"Listen Imma get on the phone real quick."

* *

*Please press one to accept this call*, said the operator.

"Hey baby. What's up."

"Just Chillin watching the Tyra show."

"You being a good girl?"

"Yeah, you know I am."

"That's what I like to hear. I got that letter from Git."

"Yeah you see Black got what he deserved?"

"That's my nigga right there. I need you to do me a favor."

"Ok, what is it?"

"How much money we got saved up?"

"Baby ever since I started dropping that extra shit I been stop counting."

"We ballin like that?"

"Yeah I just got all of it put up."

"Ok, look go to Western Union and drop $1500 in Git account."

"Alright Baby Imma get on that."

"Handle that for me bae, I love you and I'll hit you up later tonight."

"Ok, love you," replied Kristi.

"Stand by for rec!" yelled the officer.

"What you finna go do?" asked Tim, on his way to the rec yard.

"Shit let's go have a meeting real quick, then Imma work out a lil'."

After 10 minutes all the brothers were at the bench staring at Ace. The whole crew respected Ace. He came home with open arms, and made sure everybody ate.

"What's up, everybody straight?" asked Ace.

Everybody smiled and nodded in agreement. Ace looked around and saw B.B. his enforcer looking away.

"B.B. what you looking at?"

"I'm looking at those G-Mob niggaz, it look like they been getting real comfortable lately."

"Yeah man ever since they started getting a lil' money, they starting to let their nuts hang; I think they might need a wakeup call of whose pound this is," said another brother.

"Who they head is?" asked Ace.

"That nigga Stunna," replied Tim.

"I'll see 'bout that nigga."

"Other than that everybody straight?" asked Tim.

"Ok back to what yall was doing," said Ace.

Ace couldn't even work out because niggas were coming up to him like crazy. Back to back, they were dropping conformation numbers by the dozens. By now Ace was eating, he had at least 60, 000 saved up. Money was coming in so fast, thanks to that K-2. The weed and coke were still booming, but not as good as the K-2. Ace started spinning the track, something he usually does the last 15 minutes of rec to get his mind right.

*When I get out of here Imma blow*, thought Ace. His thoughts were going good until he spotted Black. *What the fuck?* Thought Ace, his eyes widening with a vengeance. "I got this nigga," Ace said to himself.

Black was standing under the hut just watching his surroundings. Ace walked around so he could sneak up behind Black. When Ace reached Black, he attacked Black like a snake at a mouse. Ace hit Black so hard behind the head it damn near knocked him out.

"Fuck nigga you thought you wouldn't see me again!" yelled Ace.

Black was on the ground balled up trying to shield his body. Ace just kept kicking. The more he thought about the 10 years the harder he kicked.

"We have a fight on the rec yard!" yelled an officer. "Stop fighting, stop fighting now!" After Ace didn't comply, 5 officers had to take physical force and sprayed them both.

"Yaaa! Yaaa!" Yelled Ace and Black. The mace was burning their eyes.

"Cuff up, cuff up!" yelled the officers. The officers cuffed them both and took them to the medical.

"Oh shit, that's Ace fighting over there," said Tim to B.B. By the time they got to the spot they were already getting cuffed up. "Now we gotta keep this shit going while bra in the box," said B.B.

"Yeah we gone hold it down," replied Tim.

* *

"Yaaa yaaa," Black was yelling in the shower.

"Shut the fuck up, puss ass nigga. Take that shit like a G."

"Fuck you nigga!" yelled Black.

"Yeah alright, you lucky I couldn't reach that thang or your ass would be getting air lifted right now," said Ace.

"Ok ladies, shut up and rinse off," said the officer.

* *

1 week later

"Checkmate," said ole man pops. That's a glove, the Michael Jackson show is on the road."

"Alright man, Pops you got that. Ace and ole man Pops were playing chess in the box, with a chessboard and pieces that ole man Pops made from scratch. The fight with Black landed them both in The Box. Ole man Pops was his bunky. They were only allowed to leave the 6 x 8 foot cell for one hour every other day to shower. "We'll play later Pops." Ace stood up to pace the cell.

"Alright, kid, anyway what's up?"

"Man, I wanna go home that's what's up."

"Don't rush it, kid. The streets ain't promised. What you plan on doing when you get out?" asked Pops.

"Man I don't know, but I know I ain't robbing no more that's for sure."

"Kid, you gotta do something positive, them white folks in that court room not sparing shit."

"Yeah I know, Pop." Ace stopped at the bars of the cell.

"So, you gotta go out there and do good. You see me I been in this shit eight times."

"Damn, Pop, you trippin'."

"Naw, it's just it was sweet back then."

"Yo Ace!" yelled Black.

"Who that is?"

"This Black."

"Man what the fuck you want?" replied Ace.

"Big bro my bad, man I don't know what I was thinking."

"Fuck that shit nigga you straight tried a nigga."

"Bra I was thinking 'bout Lil' Black."

"Shit, you couldn't been thinking that much if you right back in this bitch."

"Yea, I went back to that robbing shit and fucked up."

"Well, whatever, that's you. All I know is that it's pressure."

"Alright nigga, it is what it is."

Ace walked away from the bars and laid down thinking. *Man this my nigga but fuck 'em.*

* *

"What's good Ace," said Tim.

"Chillin', that box was hell. All I did was think about the streets."

"Yea, that's how that box will have you," replied Tim. "Anyway what's up wit that nigga you fought?"

"Man that's my CO-D, that nigga snitched on me and got me these 10 years."

"Damn. Yea, lil bra' he had to get it."

"When I get my hands on him, Imma fuck him up."

"What dorm he in?"

"I don't know, but he just got out the box with me."

"I'll find out, we gone get that snitching ass nigga from 'round here."

Ace just got out the box and was heading for his dorm. He had murder on his mind and nobody was going to stop him.

* *

"Who are you?" asked the officer.

"I'm James Thompson, I just got out the box."

"Ok, Mr. Thompson, you are on bunk 1105 L."

"Thank you." Black went over to his bunk to put everything away. Even though Black protected himself, deep down he knew, Ace wasn't nothing to fuck with.

"Aye, ain't you the one who got into that fight on the rec yard?" asked a complete stranger.

"Yea, why?"

"Well, shit. You handled yourself pretty good against those DSG niggas."

"DSG? What's that?" asked Black.

"Well, a whole bunch of down south niggas running together."

"So the dude I fought is in a gang?"

"Well, really it's an organization. But yeah, you can call it a gang."

Black sat and thought for a minute. He knew he was going to have to run with somebody. He didn't stand a chance against a whole army.

"You sound like you got pressure with those DSG niggas," said Black.

"Shit. I'm a G-Mob we got pressure wit everybody except ourselves."

"What does G-Mob stand for?"

"Gorilla Mafia, and that's why I stepped to you. You handled yourself pretty good, and you didn't back down. We need some more thoroughbreds like you."

"What, I gotta get jumped in or something?"

"Naw man just love, loyalty, and respect is all we ask for/ Plus you won't have to worry 'bout them DSG niggaz too much."

"So how do I get started?"

"Ok this what it is…"

# CHAPTER 11
# WAR

July 4 2011

Ace had been locked up for three years. Ever since Black became a G-Mob everything has been going a little crazy. The G-Mob crew respected Black and they were gonna do anything to keep their brother safe.

"You heard what happened to B.B.?" asked Tim.

"Yeah man I heard one of those G-Mob nigga stabbed him pretty good," replied Ace.

"Yea, I heard 'bout 18 times. That nigga Black came up the road and turned Gorilla overnight."

For the past couple of months DSG and G-Mob have been going to war. Whoever got caught slippin' they got it. So far, they were going blow for blow. Even though DSG was deeper and stronger, G-Mob just wouldn't back down.

"This nigga done came up here and slowed the money down. Mr. Carter been getting on my ass 'bout this shit," said Ace.

"Well you know they made Black the head, so if we get Black you know the rest of them will fall."


* *


"Got damn, P-nut, I heard you damn near killed that nigga," said Black at a G-Mob meeting.

"Hell yeah I caught that nigga in the canteen line chillin' like it's all good."

"Fuck that nigga," said Black.

"Man it's 4th of July. What we gone do for the 4th?" said one of the brothers.

"All y'all should be getting a few bottles of buck through each of yall laundry mans. They also gone have a little package for yall. Then yall will be able to get higher than a bitch!"

All the brothers shared a laugh. Buck was the prisoner way of making wine. It got you really tipsy. They took old fruits like oranges and sugar and let it sit for weeks.


* *


"Hello?"

"What's up Kris? Happy 4th," said Ace.

"Happy 4th, *Baby*!"

"What you gone do today?"

"Me and a few co-workers might go to a club or something."

"Oh yea, make sure you behave at the club."

"Boy, don't play wit me. You always saying those slick remarks like you got me in check."

"Man who the fuck you think you talking to?"

"You nigga, I've been riding with you 3 years with no problem. Nigga I been there for you, doing whatever you need me to do. And all you ever do is criticize me."

"Man listen, you trippin'."

"Naw nigga, you trippin.' If you keep this up, I don't know if Imma last too long. You gotta remember, *you* left me out here."

"You talking like I wasn't a good nigga to you out there."

"I'm not saying that, but you always accusing me of doing some shit."

"Whatever. Yo' go have fun, I'll talk to you later."

Kristi just hung up the phone without saying a word. Deep down, Ace knew he was trippin.' But he really loved Kristi, especially after she showed her loyalty.

*  *

Next morning.

"Inmate Pierre, report to the warden's office!" yelled the dorm officer. Ace had just finished eating a honey bun after doing 500 push-ups.

"Damn what you think he want?" asked Tim.

"I don't know, he probably finna cuss me out some more about all this shit that's been going on."

"Shit, just go down there and see."

"So, Mr. Pierre, I see you can't keep your brothers under control," said Mr. Carter.

"Man I don't know what's going on."

"Well word is, is that you and your brothers are beefing with the G-Mob click. I also hear that head of the G-Mob click, uhh…. James Thompson, is your homeboy from the streets and this so called beef is personal."

"Man that ain't my homeboy."

"Well, whoever the fuck he is, you two better cut it out. Lieutenant. Brown and I had to cancel 4 shipments because of the bullshit your crew has been making. Now that's a lot of money lost. See when you fuck with my money, I'll fuck with yours and I'll see to it that you get shipped way up there in the pan handle."

"Damn Mr. Carter, it ain't no need for all that. My people ain't gone drive that far."

"Ok well, you two better come to an agreement or else."

"Alright man just chill."

# Chapter 12
# Finesse Game

"Down…said….hut," Ace was a part of a flag football team and his team was pretty good.

"Touchdown!" yelled one of the inmate referees.

"Man, that's pass interference!" yelled one of the G-Mob niggaz.

Prison was a big gamble house, like a mini Las Vegas.

"Nigga I'm betting on this game, green ass nigga!" yelled P-nut to the referee.

The referee just so happened to be Tron, Ace's friend. "Who the fuck you talking to, puss as nigga?" replied Tron.

"You nigga, you blowing a nigga money!"

"Man, *fuck* your money!"

"Nigga what you wanna do?"

"Fuck nigga whatever, slide under the hut."

Ace witnessed the commotion and ran over to grab Tron.

"Nigga just chill don't crash."

"Naw man that nigga talking crazy."

"Man chill, I got this."

That night Ace had came up with a master plan and he was about to put it to work.

"Where the fuck Black at?" asked Ace.

Ace looked around until he spotted Black. Ace ripped the flags off his waistline and marched towards Black. Black witnessed everything and stood up in defense mood.

"Nigga I ain't come here for no problems. We need to have a serious talk."

"Nigga what's up."

"Spin wit' me."

"Alright what's on your mind?"

"Listen we been stabbing each other for the last couple of months. It's fucking my money up and I'm pretty sure it's fucking yours up too."

"Hell yeah my money been looking funny lately."

"Exactly. So check this out. It's time that we put this shit to the side and start getting some real money."

"What you got in mind?" asked Black.

"I was thinking wit' your crew and my crew put together we can take the whole compound by storm."

"Where exactly are you getting at?"

"Shit, instead of us beefing and slowing our money down, I was thinking we tie flags and start getting some real money."

Black stood there with a puzzled look on his face. He really didn't know what to say.

*Damn that shit sound good, but can I trust this nigga*, thought Black.

"Listen man give me a couple of days to think about it and talk to my brothers, in the meantime, holla' at your brothers and put everything to cease for the time being."

"Alright that's what it is. But I'm telling you bra, we gon' get some real money."

"Alright, Imma holla at you," replied Black.

"Man why the fuck you was over there talking to that nigga?" Tron was skeptical when Ace got back.

"Man, listen. Just chill. I talked to the nigga and we gon' put the beef to the side for right now and get some money."

"Some *money*? Man the nigga done snitched on you before trying to get some money. You don't think he will do it again?"

"Man listen, it's Ace you talking to. I know what I'm doing. Just chill, shit gone fall in my favor."

"Man that's you. I ain't fucking wit them niggas."

"Man Tron, do this for me. Trust me. It'll work out in our favor." Tron just looked at him and walked away.

* *

"Man, hell naw! I ain't fucking wit them niggas!" yelled Tim.

"Man, it's 2:30 in the morning and you doing all that fucking yelling."

"Man, I'm just telling you they got rid of a lot of our brothers and we did the same to them. What make you think they won't back stab us?"

"Listen. How long have you known me?"

"'Bout one and a half years."

"Have I steered you wrong yet?"

"No."

"Ok then. I grew up wit Black. He don't think like that. He wasn't born a leader. The only reason he joined G-Mob was for protection. You know how these puss ass niggas do it these days. They know they pussy, can't stand up for themselves, so they join a click and be someone they really not. So just chill and let me fuck this chicken."

"Alright bra, but I'm telling you, the first sign of disloyalty with anyone one of those niggas, I swear it's gonna be war."

* *

"Man, Black you trippin', fuck them niggaz," said P-nut.

"Man this a shot for us to really blow, have the whole compound on smash."

"I don't trust them niggas man, we been beefing for the last few months."

"I know Ace from the streets, even though we had our differences, he a good nigga. He bought his money."

"I don't know what type of shit you on Black, but all that tying flag shit you on, it sound like a set up to me."

"Man I'm the head of this shit. Yall gave me that position cause y'all knew I had the potential to make the right decision. Right?"

"Yeah."

"Ok then, just chill it's not gonna be a problem. Let me handle this."

"Alright big bra, I'm wit you."

It was early the next morning when Ace and Black both had their crews lined up on the benches. There were about 50 of them in all, some looking not too happy and some looking puzzled.

"Alright yall boyz all this beefing shit we gone put it to the side. Me and Black already talked and we came to an agreement that this beefing shit slowing a lot of money down."

"Yea Yeah," said Black, "we losing niggaz over some dumb shit. Instead of killing each other, let's just make some money. Think about it, we got the numbers, the rest of the clicks fear us. We can really get some money."

A lot of the brothers nodded in agreement, but P-nut just kept staring at Ace. He felt funny about this whole situation.

*I just know this nigga got something up his sleeve*, thought P-nut. Ace couldn't do anything but stare back.

"OK. So listen fellas it's official we tied flags. From now on we all brothers. We all in with each other," said Ace.

"Yeah we gon' stick together and take on any click that want it. From now on we strictly getting money," replied Black.

# CHAPTER 13
# PUTTING THE PLAN IN EFFECT

"Tighten up, Baby, the cell phone 'bout to die," said Ace.

"Boy, calm down. Ok what's the rest?"

"Uh… 9997791, that's it."

The cell phone that Sergeant Lewis gave Ace had been coming in handy. A few inmates had received more jail time because their phone calls were being monitored while they were doing money transactions. So the cell phone was a good tool.

"Alright. I got them all, Baby."

"So that's 10 different confirmation numbers, $100 a piece, so that a $1000 dollars."

"Alright I'll go pick up everything tomorrow."

"How much we got put up now?" asked Ace.

"Baby, we close to $100,000. All this money scaring me!"

"Don't worry, it's plenty more to come."

"Sorry bae for going off on you the other day. It's just you gotta understand, I've been standing strong for you, and you keep accusing me of all this bullshit."

"Man, cause I love you, and I don't wanna lose you to one of them square ass niggas."

"Lovey dovey ass nigga." whispered Tim, close by.

Ace pushed Tim away with a smile on his face.

"Bae listen. I'm a woman and you gotta understand even if I do fool around here and there, these niggaz don't mean shit. You are the one I want to be wit. My heart is with you."

Ace didn't really like what he was hearing, so he ended the conversation.

"Ok whatever you say. The phone 'bout to die. I'll call you tomorrow to check up on that."

*Beep beep*. The phone went dead.

"Oh shit. Look," said Tim. Ace looked outside and seen the truck pulling in. "Finally Mr. Carter doing his thang again."

"Yeah, he see we done stopped the madness so he can start getting money again," replied Ace.

"When I get out, I wouldn't mind knocking one of those trucks off."

"I'm telling you. But for real man, a nigga gotta go out there and do something positive. We can't keep throwing bricks at the chain game. I mean look around. This shit fucked up. These people making money off every single inmate. Don't you know we are all just a statistic?"

"Yeah, man this shit crazy."

"Yea, so we gotta get out and stay out. It ain't getting no better. It's getting worse; food fucked up, officers treating us like shit. I got four and a half years left and when I get out, I plan on being on the top of my game."

"Ok well, there go Sergeant Lewis. Go be on top of your game and get that pussy."

"Just chill, watch out for me."

Ace slipped out of the cell and right into step with the sexy sergeant.

"What's up sexy?"

"Boy, you swear you got all the game."

"Man I'm just telling you the truth; I know you got that money too?"

"Yeah, I did, and pull up your pants, boy."

"I got a little waist line, Sergeant," said Ace, and licked his lips seductively as he stared her down.

They had reached the officer's station now. Sergeant Lewis couldn't do anything but sit down and think about sex after that comment. She began to look at Ace up and down. The more she stared, the more she realized how attractive he really was. Ace was the perfect package. His waves were spinning so hard niggas hated on him. He wore a skin-tight white t-shirt that showed off all of his muscles and his V-shaped body. Sergeant Lewis got wet just imagining him between her legs. She got up and shut the officer station door behind Ace. Then, she grabbed him by the arm and led him into the officer's restroom.

*That's my dawg*, thought Tim, who had been watching the whole time from the hallway. Inside the bathroom, Sergeant Lewis pulled Ace's shorts down and started slowing sucking on his dick. Sergeant was surprised at the 9 ½ inch length that grew in her mouth. She went to work like a porn star. She sucked slow, while spitting on the head of his dick. Ace stood there with his eyes behind his head.

"Naw, get up you ain't gon' get it like that. I paid for that pussy, and that's what I want." Sergeant got up and pulled her pants down and took one leg out. Ace lifted her up and placed her on the sink. He pulled her thong to the side and entered her love zone slowly.

"Ahhh Ahhh," Sergeant Lewis moaned while squeezing his back. Aced jumped slow, wanting the moment to last forever.

"Damn this pussy so *good*," he said to her.

She replied, "Its all yours. Do what you want with it."

He lifted her legs and put his hands under her knees. Then, he sped up, trying to catch his nut before the original dorm officer came back from break. The officer yelled out that she wanted more as he hit all the right spots. Ace pumped a few more times and pulled out and nutted all over the floor. She jokingly asked if he was done and he explained that it was almost 5 years that he hadn't had any sex.

"That shit was so good! Anyway, you better clean this mess up before the officer gets back."

*   *

Everything was going as Ace had planned. They were getting double money. DSG and G Mob had the compound on smash. Everything had to go through them before anybody else got their hands on it. Ace was chain gang rich, fucking the baddest officer, had his bitch on the streets, and had the compound wrapped around his fingers. Things could not have been any better.

"I told you nigga. Shit going a lot smoother and we making way more money. As long as we keep shit going like this, by the time I get home, I'll be a millionaire."

"I don't know about millionaire, but you'll have a nice piece of change to come home to," said Black.

"How much more time you got anyway?" Ace asked Black.

"Man I fucked up and caught 30 years mandatory. It's a long story."

Ace replied in disbelief. He knew that was a lot of time to serve. Black explained his story about how he got fucked up with Spook and Puggy from the hood on a lick on a Brinks truck. "I don't know what I was thinking man," said Black. "The fucking Brinks truck driver just blew Puggy head off. I still can't believe that shit."

Ace was filled with questions and confusion and wanted answers to it all. "Ya didn't take his gun? Like how did this happen?" He asked.

Black explained he didn't see the gun. There was security in the parking lot that saw the commotion and started to come their way. He said that Spook tried to get away, but crashed into a cop car and they got caught red-handed. Ace was still shocked. He then asked about Black's family, his mother, and son.

"He's gonna be three and a half. Baby mama sent me pics. He looks just like my ass." They shared a laugh.

Ace continued, "That's good man. I couldn't imagine doing years with a son."

Black then asked about Ace's girlfriend, Kristie, and his family. Ace told him that they're good, but he hadn't gotten any visitations. He doesn't want them to see him in that condition. They both agreed. Even Black didn't want his son to see him behind prison walls.

"Man doing time is hard. It's like out of sight out of mind. People worries 'bout they self. My niggas don't even keep in touch, none of my old hoes write me. It's all good though. A nigga just gone keep pushing," Black said to Ace.

*   *

Lieutenant Brown and Warden Carter sat in Carter's office and discussed how the conditions have really cooled down with the DSG and G MOB inmates. "Inmate Pierre has done a good job controlling everything. It's something about that kid, Ace, that's different. He doesn't seem like he belongs here," Mr. Carter stated. They decided to look up his charges and were surprised to find out that he was doing time for 3 counts of armed robbery with a firearm and kidnapping. They joked around, saying that he didn't look like the type to even own a gun.

"Where's my bread, Chico?" Tim angrily confronted the man about what was owed to him.

"Yo bra, for real. I don't know what the problem is—my girl is usually on top of things." Laz, also known as Chico, was part of the Latin Pride Gang. Latin Pride consisted of Hispanics from Cuba, Puerto Rico, and Colombia just to name a few.

Tim wasn't impressed with the answer. "Aye yo, man, these excuses ain't cutting it."

"Man, nobody tryna buck you—we in this together—we stick together," said Jose, another member of the Latin Pride gang.

Their argument grew louder as Ace caught on from the other side of the dorm while getting a tattoo of Kristi's name on his wrist. "Hold on let me go see what's happening," Ace said to the person doing his tattoo before slipping out of the chair and into the hall.

As he approached, he saw that Tim and Chico were in each other's face.

"Your brother still hasn't paid me my money!" Tim said to Jose.

Jose responded, "Nigga, he told you to chill. You gotta learn to be patient!"

Suddenly, Jose pulled out a homemade knife and stabbed Tim three times.

"WETBACK!" Tim yelled out.

That got Jose so upset he reached back in his boxers and grabbed another shank and stabbed Tim three more times. Tim yelled and asked Jose to stop. Laz got in between the fight and pulled Jose off Tim.

"Yo what the FUCK!" Ace yelled. Jose explained to Ace that Tim has to watch his mouth when talking to people. The dorm was in shock as everyone stood, standing still watching what was taking place. Jose even threatened to stab Ace if he got closer. Tim stumbled up while holding his bloody wounds, trying to stop the blood.

The correctional officers charged in the room. "ok, everybody get on your racks!" Everyone rushed to their beds and awaited more instructions. One officer reported over their radio. "We have an inmate on the ground. In need of severe medical attention!"

"Yo hang in there, Tim!" Ace shouted from across the room.

"Inmate Pierre, you wanna go to the box?" asked Officer Mack.

"Man, fuck the box. Ya got the man just laying there. Do something. Fuck ass correctional officers don't give a fuck, man!," Ace responded.

Medical was already on the way to help Tim. The officer grew upset with Ace and instructed him to stand next to him. Ace went over to his bunk to put on his bobo's (shoes given to inmates) and within arms reach was the shank he always kept around for protection. As he put on his shoes, he slipped the shank into his sock. The medical staff came busting through the doors asking for the injured inmate. The nurses and officers lifted Tim on the stretcher and escorted him out.

Then, Lieutenant Brown walked through the door and just stared at the dorm. Everyone knew he didn't like when there was commotion in the compound, because it slowed down his and Carter's money. "So is anyone going to speak up and let me know what happened here?"

Nobody dared to snitch—especially on Jose, who was one of the top leaders of the Latin Pride. Everyone stood in silence. As he saw no one was cooperating he ordered a strip search.

"Everyone strip down to your boxers and form a line starting with this row here," said Officer Mack. Inmates mumbled their disapproval of the strip search, but complied.

"Take all your sheets off the bed and spread them across the bed," ordered Lieutenant Brown.

"You guys know the procedure! Line up at the showers, put your hands up, open your mouth, drop your boxers and lift those nuts," officer Kneal demanded.

The inmates did not like officer Kneal. There was just something about him. The way he would look at them was weird. The first row of inmates followed directions as they squatted and coughed. Officer Kneal just left them squatting there and continued staring at their asses, which is something Melbo didn't like.

"Yo what's up, officer Kneal, we done? You keep looking and shit!" Melbo was an average inmate, but he couldn't stand for Officer Kneal's staring. Officer Kneal didn't like Melbo questioning him..

"You know what inmate Harris? Out of the showers and pack your belongings. You're going to the box for disrespect."

"Faggot!" Melbo whispered under his breath as an officer escorted him away.

"Next Row of Inmates into the shower!" Officer Mack yelled.

As the next row walked up, Jose passed Ace with a smirk on his face. Instantly Ace swung with everything in him. Jose's nose was broken from that one blow.

"Fuck ass wetback! You got my brother messed up!" Ace screamed.

Jose fell to the floor, yelling from the pain. as Ace stomped and kicked him. Officer Mack rushed over and pulled Ace off Jose. "What the hell are you guys problem?" asked officer Mack. "You guys finish here I'm going to take care of this", said Lt Brown. Ace was escorted out to the box.

"Pierre what the hell you got going on?" Lieutenant Brown stated. Ace ignored him and proceeded to walk. Lieutenant Brown asked again and once again, Ace ignored him and kept walking.

"Process him as soon as possible. Write up a fighting Disciplinary Report," Lieutenant Brown said to the intake officer. Over the radio Lieutenant Brown ordered Officer Mack to get the dorm cleaned and the inmates in their bunk for the rest of the day.

"Okay, you're going in here," the intake officer said to Ace. He dropped his bag with his belongings in it and laid down. He stared at the bottom of the top bunk and instantly fell asleep.

# CHAPTER 14
# ROUGH TIMES

"Oh shit! Fuck yeah. Right there. Right there!" yelled Kristi.

*WAP! WAP!* Fat Boy slapped Kristi's ass.

"Damn girl. Throw that shit back," said Fat Boy.

"Uh Uh! Yes! Yes!" yelled Kristi.

Fat Boy was slow stroking Kristi's wet pussy from the back while he played with her clit at the same time.

"You like that shit baby?" asked Fat Boy.

"Oh my God. Yes. I'm about to cum. Don't stop!" Fat Boy broke down as he ejaculated all over Kristie's back.

"Man, *what the fuck!*" Ace jumped out of his sleep. He dreamed that his homeboy Fat Boy was fucking his girl Kristi. Ace had been in the box for 20 days. He was sentenced to 30 days. All he could do was think about his family and how he didn't receive letters from anyone; it was killing him. The officers would pass out mail and skip his room everyday. This is when he realized the truth behind the phrase "Out of sight, out of mind."

"15,16,17,18,19,20…" Ace was counting his pushups. Inmates barely eat anything in the box, so they had to workout out, or they would end up leaving the box a lot smaller than they went in.

"Knock. Knock, knock, inmate Pierre," the mail officer said.

Ace jumped up quick. "Yeah that's me."

The mail officer kicked the mail under the door.

*Finally! Damn. Wonder who this is,* Ace thought to himself.

*Yo bro whats up. It's Tron and Troub.. hope you doing good in there. We just out here holding it down. Everything is everything. Troub told me to tell you keep your head up. You know that boy go home next month. He happy as hell. Just keep your head up and we'll see when you get out. Oh yea, they shipped Jose, so you don't gotta worry bout that wetback no more. A couple fights went down with the brothers and the Latins, but its all good now. Aiight, Peace. Love.*

Ace threw the letter. He was really hoping to hear from a family member or close friend.

*Man this shit crazy. So everybody out there really go days without thinking to send me a kite? I gotta get out this place.* Ace had about 4 years left and it seemed so long. He was going through the roughest times. You couldn't leave your room at all—only to take 2 minute showers, then back to the cells. *I'll be a convicted felon when I get out, I need a plan. I can't fail. I have to succeed*, he thought to himself. Ace had 5 brothers. He was the second oldest, he hadn't heard from any of them. Not his mom or dad. It was killing him that he couldn't be there for his brothers. He would always think if somebody tried to mess with his brothers, he wouldn't be able to protect them. Ace's eyes just swelled with tears as he went deep into thought.

"Pierre, pack it up! Time to get out of this place," said the intake officer.

"Finally man! I'm ready to eat."

Ace had lost about 8 pounds in the box. Everyone hated the box, but if you had to go, then you had to go. Ace got out of the box and went straight to the yard.

"Yo Troub, what's good?"

"What's up homie? You finally out I see," he said to Ace.

"Yeah man that shit was hell bro. I gotta stay out that shit."

"Yeah man that shit can drive a nigga crazy," replied Troub.

As usual, Inmates were doing everything on the yard. There were guys running around the track, gangs in small groups, soccer games, football games, and officers walking around monitoring the inmates. But the most popular place was the cage. The cage always had the most inmates in it. The cage consisted of a few pull-up bars, push-up bars, and dip bars. It was Ace's favorite place to be. Ace ended his convo with Troub and walked toward the cage. He couldn't wait to get started.

"1,2,3,4,5,6,7…" Ace sounded off on the pull-up bars. He jumped down after doing just 7. The box had him a little weak.

*Man I was able to do 15 straight before, I gotta catch back up,* thought Ace. His usual routine was just to hit every exercise in a circle. It would be a full workout for the body. He went from pull-ups to push-ups to dips. When Ace was done he was sore as hell. He thought to himself that he just finished a good workout when the whistle rang across the yard for everyone to return to their dorms.

"Yo Ace!" Tron and Troub yelled out.

"What's up, yall boys." Ace said. They headed back to their dorms.

# CHAPTER 15
# MIDWAY POINT

1 ½ years later—August 2012.

Things were the same at Ham C.I. Ace was still doing him with Lieutenant Brown and Warden Carter. Troub and Tron were still there hanging on strong. Kristi was still there for Ace, but had been acting kinda funny lately. Black was still around and he still had his crew on lock. Everything was the same. The time was still killing Ace but, with only had 2 ½ years left, he had to hang in there. In prison, they called you a short timer with time like that left. You also had to look out, because other inmates who were jealous would do anything to jeopardize that.

"Lets keep the line moving," ordered the cafeteria officer. Ace looked down at his plate and wondered what he was eating. The food in the department of corrections was horrible. They didn't care about the inmates. The plate consisted of a half-cooked hot dog, 2 cold slices, of bread, and some watery peas and carrots.

"Grown ass men just came from working out in the hot ass sun and this what yall feed us?" Ace said out loud.

"Stay out prison and you wont have that problem," said the officer and kept it moving. Ace sat at the table with Tron.

"Aye yo, wassup? You heard from Troub since his last letter?"

"No. He should be doing good though. You know Troub smart enough," Tron said.

"I'll write his mom tonight," said Ace.

"Okay this row. Your time is up. Lets go!" yelled an officer.

"Alright bro. I'll see you later on the yard," said Tron. The two marched to throw their trays away.

"Stop fighting! Get the fuck down!" yelled a correctional officer.

Ace and Tron looked back and saw two inmates going at it. One inmate was bleeding really bad from his side.

"Damn it look like he got stabbed," Ace said. The cafeteria was full of commotion. Inmates were moving out the way as other officers stormed the cafeteria, spraying mace.

"Get the fuck down! Get down!" yelled the officers.

"Man that shit is crazy!" Tron said as he and Ace exited the cafeteria.

"See that's why we gotta get out of here safe, Bro," said Ace.

"Yeah, this shit crazy. I'm really trying to get home the way I came in," replied Tron.

"This shit is hell man. This shit literally the step before death. I miss my people man, I never thought I would be going through this shit," said Ace.

"Yeah man, you basically dead to the world. Man, we gone be good. We just gotta get out and do better. Besides Ace, you seem smart, man. I just like the way you move. I never told you this, but I like the way you came in and stayed true."

# CHAPTER 16
# MAKE A WAY

"Bout 2 years left, Baby," said Kristi.

"Yeah I know man, can't wait," replied Ace.

"I can't wait too, Baby Boy."

"What you been up too, what's new?" asked Ace.

"Same ole, just maintaining. Missing you."

"I miss my brothers, man."

"They ok. I seen TJ in the club. He all grown up, got a beard and all," said Kristi.

"Haha, hell naw! For real?"

"Yes, and he had all the girls too,"

"That's crazy, can't wait to see them boys,"

"Baby, I have something to tell you," said Kristi.

Ace just shook his head because he never wanted to hear those words.

"What happened Kristi?"

"I was pregnant."

"Huh? You *was* pregnant? As in past tense?"

"Yes, *was* pregnant. I got an abortion."

"When were you planning on telling me this, Kristi?"

"I was just waiting for the right time. I didn't want to make your time any harder than it is."

"So, why you got an abortion?"

"What you mean *why I got an abortion*? I didn't mean for this to happen," said Kristi.

"Then, why you got your legs open in the first place?" yelled Ace.

"Baby, you left me out here. I'm holding you down. You expect me to keep my legs closed for *10 years*, Jerrell? What am I suppose to do? I'm a woman. I have needs," said Kristi.

Ace just sat on the phone shaking his head. "So you been fucking a bitch ass nigga in the crib round all that money and shit? What if this nigga know something?"

"He don't know shit, Jerrell. Besides all the money is at my mom's house, in a safe under her bed,"

"So when the fuck all this happened? When the fuck did you meet another nigga?"

"I've been talking to him for about a year now, nothing serious,"

"Nothing *serious*?" yelled Ace. "But you out here getting pregnant."

"I'm so sorry, Baby. He means nothing to me. Just someone I'm passing time with. I just miss you so much!" cried Kristi.

Ace hated to hear Kristi cry. He really had to think about it, because what she was saying was true. He had left Kristi for a decade and he couldn't expect her not to move on just a little.

"Kristi, this too much. We gotta talk later,"

"I'm so sorry, Baby," cried Kristi.

Ace just hung up the phone and went to lay down. He knew he was going to be stressing for atleast                a                week.


*   *


"REC YARD! REC YARD!" yelled the officer.

Ace jumped up from his nap at the sound of the yelling. He had become a light sleeper over the years. You had to sleep light in this place. It was liable to go down at any time.

"I know you sliding, Ace," said his bunky.

"Yeah, I'll go out there," replied Ace. He put on his shoes and quickly brushed his teeth  and headed out the door. As Ace walked to the rec yard, he couldn't stop thinking about what Kristi told him. *Can't believe this*, he thought. Once at the cage, he settled into his workout routine.

"10,11,12,13,14,15....whew!" yelled Ace.

"You got those pull-ups down pat I see.".

Ace looked back to see it was P Nut. Now, even though DSG and G MOB had tied flags and had an understanding, Ace still stayed away from a few of them; especially P-Nut, the G MOB member who'd stabbed BB a few years back.

"Yea, I do a little something," said Ace.

"Shit, I need to start working out with you," said P Nut.

"Well I'm here everyday," replied Ace.

"Cool, but listen man, your name Jerrell right?"

"Why? Who wants to know?"

"I do," said P Nut.

"Why the hell you want to know my name? replied Ace.

"Well, I already know that's your name. I see it on your I.D. all the time,"

"So, why the hell you asking if that's my name then?."

"Well, to be honest, you know me and Black are in the same dorm. The other day, before we went to dinner, he told me to close his locker. So I went over to close it and seen his paperwork,"

Ace's eyes just widened. "Ok?" said Ace.

"What you mean, ok?" replied P-Nut.

"You seen his paper work, ok. What's the big deal?"

"He snitched on you, Jerrel. That's the big deal. I was like, you mean to tell me the head of G MOB is a fucking snitch? The man I been listening to is a snitch!" said P-Nut.

Ace just looked at P-Nut. "Yes, the Nigga snitched on me," said Ace.

"So you know that? And you got this nigga walking round with his chest poking out like he ain't a *rat*?"

"It's not that Nut. It's a lot going on you don't know about,"

"I don't care what's going on. He is a fucking snitch— period!"

"I feel you. But trust me, it's more to it," replied Ace.

"Well you gotta fill me in and let me know why I've been answering to a snitch for a while now."

Ace just sighed. "Alright, let's walk the track," said Ace. Black eyed from the sidelines as the two of them walked and talked the track...

"What Ace and P-Nut got going on?" asked Black.

" I don't know," said G Baby. G Baby was the youngest G MOB member. He usually stayed under Black.

"Ace never talk to nobody. That's weird," said Black.

"You gotta holla at P-Nut and ask him,"

"I'm going to alright."

"So yeah. There you have it. That's why you've been answering to a snitch all this time," said Ace.

"Damn, you turned that situation into a good one. I would of just killed his ass and made the situation much easier," said P Nut.

"You can't always think like that. You gotta think first P-Nut. Me doing anything to him would have just made my time harder. I had to think of another way," replied Ace.

"Ace Man, I like you. You just made snitching not seem bad. I hate snitches," said P-Nut.

"Naw man. It's definitely bad, but it's done now. So I had to think for myself,"

"Well listen, the secret's out and I'm not answering to no snitch."

"Just chill, P-Nut. Just play it cool,"

"I'll kill that Nigga if you want me to," said P-Nut.

Ace just stared in a glaze. He was thinking about the hell Black had put him through all these years. He wanted to give P-Nut the green light, but his heart couldn't let him.

"Just chill, P-Nut. Give me a couple of days to think about it," said Ace.

"Well, while you thinking, Imma be staying far away from that nigga. I might end up slapping him."

"Hahaha! Damn bra, you gotta learn self-control."

"I am! I'm about to self-control myself from killing this nigga!"

*Brrrr. Brrrr.* Time to go in fellas!" yelled the rec officer.

"Aight, P Nut, I'm going to have something for you later. In the meantime, just chill please," said Ace.

P-Nut just nodded and walked off.

# CHAPTER 17
# THIRD QUARTER

"Inmate Pierre," said the officer over the loud speaker. Ace walked over to the window.

"Lieutenant Brown would like to see you," said the officer.

Ace went to get into his class A uniform to head out to Lieutenant Brown's office.


"What's up Lieutenant.," said Ace.

"Good, good. How have *you* been?"

"I'm good Lieutenant, just maintaining," replied Ace.

"I see you're basically in the 3rd quarter of your time."

"Yea, I'm almost there Lieutenant,"

"Well listen, you're a short timer. I thought I'll send you to another camp."

"Another camp?" asked Ace.

"Yes another camp,"

"Why? I'm good here Lieutenant. I'm comfortable."

"And that's exactly why I'm moving you," said the Lieutenant. "You see this isn't a place for you to get comfortable. God just sent you here for you to learn a lesson. For you to learn life. Never get too comfortable. Change is always good,".

Ace just sat there and thought about what he'd just heard. "Well where do you plan on sending me?" he asked finally.

"Well, we have a few faith-based camps you can choose from."

"Faith-based camp? What is that?"

"They are camps with different programs and religious studies. You don't have to attend the religious studies, but they have all sorts of different programs you can get into. They help prepare you for the streets," said Lieutenant Brown.

*Fuck it! I'm tired of this shit anyway,* thought Ace. *Might as well switch it up right quick.* "Aight, why not," he said.

"I can have you shipped out by next week. I like you, Inmate Pierre. I see something in you. I want to give you this opportunity to THINK. You're young, you have a long life ahead of you. Think of something. Anything is possible," said the Lieutenant.

"Thanks Lieutenant. I don't see why not. What about captain, and everything you guys got going on?" asked Ace.

"We'll be okay. We are about to shut things down anyway. Feels like it's getting a little hot," said the Lieutenant.

"Ohhh, so yall not getting comfortable?" asked Ace.

"EXACTLY," he said. "Exactly."

*  *

Later that day, P-Nut was at the cage like clockwork.

"What's up P-NUT," said Ace.

"Chilling man. Shit's been real weird since you told me what you told me about Black."

"At least you been keeping your self-control. I don't want him to know what I got going on. He already a snitch," replied Ace.

"Yeah I feel you, I just can't stand that snitching shit, plus he walking 'round here like a boss. He really pussy," said P-Nut.

"Hahaha! You gotta' learn to *chill*."

"Naw man. I take things like that serious," replied P-Nut.

"Well listen Lieutenant trying to ship me out."

"Damn. Why?"

"Well, I only got 'bout 2 years left, and he just want me to get my mind together before I go home."

"That's good Bro. Fuck it. Leave."

"I am, might as well," said Ace.

Ace wasn't planning to tell anybody about his departure. Prison can get so slimey, you just couldn't trust anyone. "Don't tell nobody either," said Ace.

"Nigga, you see I hate snitches. What I look like doing it?" replied Black.

They both shared a laugh.

Just then, Black walked up behind Ace and P-Nut.

"What's up with yall two?" asked Black.

"Just spinning the track. What's up with you?" asked Ace.

"Nothing. I been seeing you guys hangout a lot lately," said Black.

"And so what?" said P-Nut.

"Yo, who the hell you talking to?" said Black.

"You, nigga," replied P-Nut.

Ace got in between the two. "Ya. Chill, man. What the hell y'all got going on?"

"I don't know what's up with this nigga," said Black.

"Y'all just chill. P-Nut, let me holla at Black right quick," said Ace.

P-nut looked at Black hard before turning and walking away.

"What's up with that nigga?" asked Black.

"He just stressed, Bra. He miss his people and shit. You know how that be."

"Man, he better come correct before he gets flipped out here."

"Chill, no need for that. It's not that serious. Everybody go through it."

"Yeah, whatever," replied Black.

"Listen man, I might be stepping down," said Ace.

"What you mean stepping down?"

"You know, I'll be going home soon. So I just want to chill out for a little bit. Give someone else the spot. I'll watch them, making sure they're keeping it together."

"Yeah, I feel you. I just hope it's someone that can hold it down like you can," said Black.

"Trust me, everything will be ok. Everything will still run the same. Only thing that might change is me getting the work."

"What you mean? So the operation getting shut down?"

"Yeah, as far as us still being the main people to buy drugs from. My plug calling it quits," replied Ace.

"Damn, that's crazy. I mean that's how everybody was eating."

"I know, but I gotta respect my people. It's out of my hands. I mean you still got visitation. It won't be as much, but it'll still get the job done," said Ace.

"Yeah, you right. Now I just gotta find somebody brave enough to bring it," replied Black.

"Yeah, that's the problem. Well, it's out my hands. I'll be going home soon, so I can't be involved with that shit."

"You right, you don't want to loose any gain time," replied Black.

*Brrr, Brrr.* The rec whistle went off.

"Aiight. See you later, Man," said Black.

"Ok, catch up," replied Ace and took off for the cell.

"Yo P-Nut!" Peanut looked back to see Ace calling his name.

"Yo what's up Ace."

"Haha, you almost went off back there. I had to throw the nigga off."

"Man fuck that nigga! I can't believe this nigga been a snitch the whole time," replied P-Nut."

"That's how it go, Bra. Your worst enemy can be right next to you. You'll never know who's who. But one thing about it, what happens in the dark will always come to light," said Ace.

"He just so fake, Man. That shit bothers me."

"Fuck that nigga. Me playing it how I played it is what got everybody doing good, and the compound calm. Gotta keep your enemies close, Nut."

"I feel you. But I'm not with all that thinking shit. I just want to flip his ass."

"Hahaha! Nut, you a handful! But listen, I'll be gone soon, so let me get your info. I'll send you something to make sure you're good. Things are gonna slow down, money wise. My plug pulling the plug," said Ace.

"Damn, that sucks. Aight, write this shit on your hand," replied P-Nut. P-Nut wrote his info onto Ace's hand.

"Cool, I got you. Just look out for it," said Ace.

"Will do. Yo, Ace, appreciate it man. You taught me a few things since you've been here. While you gone I promise to keep this going," said P-Nut.

"Listen, just promise to keep your head up, move safe, and make it home safe," said Ace.

P-nut just smiled. They dapped each other up and went separate ways.

# CHAPTER 18
## ANOTHER BEGINNING

*Doom! Doom!, Doom!"* The dorm officer was kicking the side of Ace's bunk. "Mr. Pierre! Get up, pack it up. It's time to go."

Ace got up and knew exactly where he was going.

"Aight officer let me get my things together," replied Ace.

"Ok, you have 30 minutes," replied the officer. Ace sat up on the bed, grabbed his toothbrush, and went to brush his teeth.

*Aight Ace, it's almost 4th quarter, you got this. You've made it this far, soon you'll be reunited with your family again.* Those were the thoughts going through Ace's head. Ace sat back on his bunk to get his belongings together.

"You out of here, Kiddo," said the old man next to Ace.

"Yeah. I'm gone Unc."

"You know where you going?"

"Naw, not yet, Unc."

"Ok, be cool youngin'. Oh yeah, Ace, remember this: IT'S NOT OVER YET. YOU STILL HAVE A LONG LIFE. MAKE THE MOST OF IT. ANYTHING YOU PUT YOUR MIND TO YOU CAN DO."

Ace just looked back. "Thanks Unc, I needed to hear that," replied Ace.

"That's my job, kiddo, be safe."

Ace gathered the rest of his things and went out the door.

*　*

August 2013 – 1 year later

"15, 16, 17, 18, 19, 20…" Ace was counting his dips. It had been a year since he'd been at the new camp. He liked it. It was quiet and he enjoyed going to the different programs they offered.

"Zoe sak passé," said Jean. Jean was an older Haitian dude Ace met when he first arrived there.

"Zoe. What's good," replied Ace.

"Man, you got *big*. When you get home you gonna' have all the girls," said Jean.

"Hahaha!" they both laughed.

"Naw, but listen, that cell phone should be coming in tonight. So if you need it let me know," said Jean.

"Alright. I'll let you know. Matter of fact, I will need it. I need to get in contact with my brothers," replied Ace.

"Okay. I will send it through the laundry man."

"OK, cool. Now finish up these sets with me. Told you, you gotta start working out ZOE."

"Yeah yeah, whatever," replied Jean.

The next day, Ace got his brother's number from Kristi. He dialed the number on the cell phone Jean sent over.

"Hello," answered TJ.

"Hello TJ. What's good? It's Ace."

"Damn! What's up big bro? How you been?"

"Man I been good, what's up with the family?" asked Ace.

"Everything good. You know Grandma died."

"Yeah. I know man. It's killing me I couldn't be at the funeral."

"It's cool tho. She watching over us," replied TJ. "How you calling me anyway?"

"A dude I'm cool with got a cell phone in here."

"Cell phone, how the hell?"

"Long story, TJ, just know this is a world of its own, and I don't ever want to see you in here," replied Ace.

"Man, you don't gotta worry about me. That's one place I know I'm not going to meet," replied TJ.

"That's what I like to hear. So what you been up to? What's new?"

"I been chilling man. I'm in Tallahassee now."

"Oh Yeah? How is it up there?"

"Living expenses cheap. Not as fast as Miami, but it's cool."

"What's with Dad? He okay?"

"Yeah. I talked to him the other day. He said Sticks bad as hell," replied Ace. Sticks was Ace's other little brother.

"Oh yeah? What he been doing?"

"I don't know. Dad just said he tired of that shit."

"Damn, I miss the ole boy."

"We miss you too bro," said TJ. "When you coming home?"

"I only have 'bout a year left."

"That's it? Man you'll be home in a blink of an eye."

"Yeah I know. I can't wait. But look bro, they' bout to do count. I'll call you later."

"Aight big bro, keep your head up."

"Aight LOVE."

"LOVE," replied TJ.

Ace hung up the phone, took the battery out, and hid the phone. He was so happy to talk to his brother. He knew this last year was going to fly by.

*   *

"Yo Black, I don't like how shit been going since Ace been gone. You running all over everybody like we all not brothers," said Tron.

Ace had left the head position of DSG to Tron. Tron had been there the whole time, so he knew how things were supposed to go.

"I'm trying the best I can, Tron. What you want me to do?" asked Black.

"Listen. I don't know what you and Ace had going on. But, as of today, we just gonna untie flags. You G-Mob niggas can do yall. This too much. Seems like only Ace can hold this shit down," said Tron.

"Man whatever. You pulling on Ace dick and shit."

"Nigga, it's not my fault niggas don't listen to you. I don't think this position really fit you, but that's not my problem. I'm DSG, so we gon' be good," said Tron.

"If that's how you want it, then it is what it is," replied Black.

P-nut was just sitting on the bench listening to the conversation. He was so mad at what just happened. After he found out Black was a snitch he really wanted to be a part of DSG.

Tron just walked away. Even some of the G-Mob members walked away. A lot of them had built real relationships with some of the DSG members, so they weren't really happy with the decision.

# CHAPTER 19
# FOURTH QUARTER

6 months later.

Ace was up to 180 pounds solid. He had been going extra hard on the exercises since he had a little bit of time left.

"Yeah boy, you ready for them streets," said Jean.

"Yeah man. I can't wait. I never thought I'd have 6 months left."

"You talking like you caught a life sentence," replied Jean.

"Yeah I know, but you know how that shit go. This shit be having you feel like you gonna be here forever," said Ace.

"Yeah I know. Shit. I got 4 years left and it feel like forever."

"Damn 4 years? I hate how the system got so many good niggas locked up in this shit."

"Yeah lil' bro, that's how it go. It's their world. We just live in it," replied Jean.

"So what you plan on doing when you get out?" asked Jean.

"I don't know man. Kinda want to write a book or something."

"A book? *Sacré bleu!* You cannot write no damn book!" laughed Jean.

"You crazy. Why not? I got a story to tell."

"Naw, I'm just messing with you. You can do whatever you wanna do."

"Thanks Jean. Or maybe be a personal trainer or something," replied Ace.

"Yeah. That sounds more like it, haha!"

"You know what? I'm going to write that book since you want to be funny and shit."

"I believe you, lil' bro, the shit just sound funny to me."

"Well, keep laughing. I'm going to be the next big author on yo' ass."

"Okay, just when you make it, don't forget 'bout me."

"FUCK You!" replied Ace as they both shared a laugh.

* *

"What the hell!" yelled Tron.

He woke up from his sleep to the sound of commotion outside. From his window he saw a

SWAT team rushing the buildings Mr. Carter and Lieutenant Brown had the trucks drop the product to.

"Move, move, move!" yelled one of the SWAT officers.

"Damn, I thought Ace said they was going to call it quits. Looks like they couldn't't stop," thought Tron. He watched as the officers brought out boxes and boxes filled with different drugs.

"Is that all the boxes, Officer Jennings?" asked a SWAT officer.

"Yes captain," replied Jennings.

"Well, well, well, this has to be one of our biggest busts in prison history," said the SWAT Captain.

"Yeah. They really had an organization going on. OVER 100 pounds of cocaine," replied Jennings.

The inmates watched as Mr. Carter and Lieutenant Brown were escorted out the building. They couldn't believe what they were seeing. The compound was in a frenzy and would definitely be shut down for the rest of the day.

*Now we gotta be in this shit for the rest of the day*, thought Tron. Just before he backed away from the window, Tron saw the side doors of one of the buildings open. He couldn't believe what he was witnessing. Black was being escorted out by one of the officers.

*Bitch ass nigga!* thought Tron and immediately pulled out paper and pen to write Ace a letter.

* *

"What's up Kristi, what you up to?" asked Ace.

"Nothing, same ole, just got back from work."

"How was it?"

"It was good," replied Kristi. "Baby you only got a few more months left," she said.

"I can't wait. It actually feels like it's taking longer to be honest. This is the longest part."

"Ace, I'm 3 months pregnant," blurted Kristi.

"Repeat that."

"I said, I'm pregnant!" She burst out crying.

Ace's heart dropped. He ended up forgiving Kristi's first pregnancy, but this was too much. "So you couldn't learn to protect yourself after the first time?"

"I don't know how it happened, Jerrell. It just happened," replied Kristi.

"So what happened to the abortion?"

"Jerrell, do you know how hard it was for me the first time? I killed a human. It ruined me. I can't go through that twice!" she cried.

Ace just stayed silent on the phone. After a minute, he told Kristi he would talk to her later. "Wait before you go here's my homie P-Nut's info, drop 500 in his account for me," said Ace. He gave her the info and hung up.

*　*

"Mail call! Mail call!" Yelled the dorm officer. Everybody got quiet. The inmates took mail call very seriously. Didn't want anyone *not* hearing their name. "Davis, Williams, Jones, Pierre—"

Ace jumped up to get his mail. "I hope none of these hoes writing me now that I'm 'bout to go home," thought Ace.

Ace grabbed the envelope. The envelope read Ms. Durant. *Ms. Durant*, thought Ace. He ripped open the letter.

*Hey fam, what's up? It's Tron, you already know. Just hitting you up. I'm still at home doing pretty good. A few things changed since you went away. We don't mess with those boys on the other block any more.*

Ace knew he was referring to DSG and G-Mob.

*Things got sore, so we let it go. Hope you doing good. Listen remember when you told me those 2 old heads from 85th street were gonna get out the game? Well they didn't, they kept going, and the FBI rushed their house. They got a lot of shit out the house. It was crazy. The block been hot ever since. Then guess who I seen getting dropped off down the street? Black nigga. Yeah Black. You get the picture. SNAKE! Hope you doing good keep your head up homie.*

Tron sent the letter to his mom first. Then she sent it to Ace. Inmates weren't allowed to directly write each other. Although Tron was writing in code Ace knew exactly what he was saying and he couldn't believe it.

*This nigga Black tripping now, he a real life snake*, thought Ace.

# CHAPTER 20
# DON'T LOOK BACK

Ace was sitting in a "RE-ENTRY" program just think of everything he'd gone through. "Thank you Lord, for letting me get through this situation. Thank you Lord, for keeping me safe. Thank you for keeping my family safe."

"Mr. Pierre wake up," said Mr. Duncanson, the group leader.

"I wasn't sleep," replied Ace.

"Your eyes were closed, you were asleep. Ok, listen up. When you guys get out there, things are going to be a lot different. You guys will be convicted felons, and you're black, so that's two strikes against you," said Mr. Duncanson.

"Man, the system just lock us up and take away everything from us and expect us not to go back to the same ole shit," said Ace.

"The government could care less what you do after this. They basically half way got you. It's on you to get out and prove them wrong," replied Mr. Duncanson.

"Man, I'm not worried 'bout coming back. They can have this shit," said Ace.

"Ok I'm going to play this small clip of previous inmates and their testimonies," said Mr. Duncanson.

Mr. Duncanson flipped on the television as the inmates watched. Ace pulled out a piece of paper and pen and wrote a letter to P-Nut.

*"Yo NUT, what's good? It's Ace…"*

* *

"You almost gone, ZOE," said Jean.

"Yea, I know man. It's over with," replied Ace.

"What's the first thing you going to eat?"

"Some pussy! Hahaha!"

"I know that's right, my nigga," replied Jean. "Naw bro, when you get out you handle certain things. You got to get your ID and register yourself with the police department," he continued.

"Yeah, I know man. I just want to get out this shit."

"Man, you there. You have nothing to worry about it. Just get out and do right. Definitely don't go out there robbing people and shit again."

"Hell naw, nigga. I'm never doing that shit again."

"You better not. You'll find yourself with a life sentence," replied Jean.

"Naw. my *family* way more important than that," said Ace.

*     *

"Yo Nut! You got mail!" yelled another inmate. P-nut wasn't used to getting mail. He got up quick and raced his way towards the officer station. He grabbed the letter and it read Mrs. Pierre. Nut knew it was from Ace. He ripped the letter open and began to read, *Yo NUT....*

*     *

Release Date 8-29-14

"Chow, chow, chow!" the officer yelled for the inmates to get up and eat breakfast. P-nut got up and got dressed and exited the dorm. "Chow, chow chow!" yelled the dorm officer. "Time for breakfast ladies."

You didn't have to attend breakfast you didn't want to. It was optional. Black looked up from under the covers and gave another inmate a sign as everybody left the dorm.

*Slurp, slurp.* came the sounds of Black getting head from another inmate.

"Ohhh shit yeah. Just like that, Bitch," Black moaned.

"Mmm mmm." The inmate had a mouth of Black, and Black was thoroughly enjoying it.

P-nut crept to Black's dorm during movement for breakfast. He ducked down, so the officer couldn't see him through the booth. P-nut looked around but he didn't see anyone. "Mmm mmm," the inmate performing oral sex let out a few moans. P-nut looked back towards the stalls and saw someone on their knees.

*What the fuck?* thought P-Nut and walked towards the back. He pulled out his shank before he turned the corner. "Get your faggot ass up!" said P-Nut.

The inmate quickly got up and ran out the bathroom without saying a word. "Yo, what the hell, P-Nut!" yelled Black.

"You a snitch and a faggot, you gotta go," whispered P-Nut. Then he lunged at Black and stabbed him continuously.

"Ahhh!" yelled Black.

P-nut had stabbed him 4 times in the neck before Black could get out his second scream. P-nut stabbed him about 16 times in the upper body area and quickly ran out the door. The dorm officer thought he'd heard a scream and came out of the booth. The officer circled the dorm, but didn't see anything. Right before the officer stepped back into the booth, he spotted a body lying in the corner of his eye. "OH MY GOD!" yelled the officer.

He quickly grabbed his radio and called for backup.

* *

Ace hadn't slept all night, he couldn't wait for them to call his name. Some inmates were still at breakfast, but Ace didn't go. He wanted to be starving by the time they released him.

"Inmate Pierre, time to go," said the dorm officer.

Ace kind of froze up. He never thought he would hear those words. It had finally hit him. Ace already had his things packed.

"Finally gone, right?" said the dorm officer.

"Yeah. I'm finally gone," replied Ace.

"Before I let you go, remember not everybody makes it out of here. You are blessed, remember that."

"Thank you," replied Ace.

Ace just exited the dorm and started marching his way to the front of the building where he would be released.

As he walked he just kept thinking of everything that had transpired over the years. *Thank the Lord I made it out.* Ace couldn't wait to see his family when he got home. *I gotta MAKE A WAY, no matter what, I can't let this stop me*, thought Ace.

"Mr. Pierre," said the release officer. Ace jumped up to get his bus pass.

"Miami, right?" said the officer.

"Yes ma'am," replied Ace.

"Hey did you guys hear about that murder at Ham C.I.?" said another officer.

"Yeah, I heard the inmate was stabbed several times," replied the officer. The officer looked towards Ace and the other inmates being released. "You guys are lucky to make it out. Go out there and make your parents proud. If you have kids, be there for your kids. This isn't the place for a person."

The inmates just took everything in. Ace heard what they said about Ham C.I., but showed no emotion.

The officer walked the inmates to the back door. The men couldn't wait to see the sunlight on the other side. The officer opened the door and it felt like he opened the door to the gates of heaven. Ace took his first step of freedom.

"Good luck to you guys!" yelled the officer. "DON'T LOOK BACK!"

The inmates did just that. Ace was still in shock. The now former inmates walked to the bus stop and waited. One dude that Ace usually saw in the cage, but never talked to, walked towards him. "What's up, Ace. I didn't know you were going home."

"Yes. I just kept quiet about it. You know how that can be," replied Ace.

"So what's next for you? What you gonna do Ace?"

Ace looked at the inmate and replied "Make a way…"

# ABOUT THE AUTHOR

Jamie Francois is a Haitian-American, born and raised in Miami, fl. His parents, originally from Haiti, moved to Miami when they were younger, and had 6 boys. Jamie is the second oldest. Life wasn't always great for him and his family but his parents always found a way to keep them up to date. Jamie's parents are his biggest motivation. Through them he learned that you can make a Way out of no way. On spare time Jamie likes to play basketball, travel, and hang out with friends. With this being his first released book he's looking to make his mark in the literature world with plenty more books to come...

# Book Order Form

Please print this form and mail with your check or money order, payable to:

Make A Way Publications
810 SW 102nd Terrace Unit 101
Pembroke Pines, Florida, 33025
Tel: (305) 988-7031
Email: makeawaypub@gmail.com

*Books will be mailed through regular postal mail media. Delivery may require 2- 3 weeks*

| Quantity | Book Title | Cost | Total |
|---|---|---|---|
|  | The Step Before Death $14.99 |  |  |
| Add | U.S Add $4, Outside US $10 Shipping & Handling per book |  |  |
|  | Total Submitted |  |  |

| Ship to | |
|---|---|
| Name: |  |
| Address: |  |
| City, State and ZIP |  |
| Telephone No.: |  |
| Email Address: |  |

Thank you for your business!

# BOOK ORDER FORM

Please print this form and mail with your check or money order, payable to:

Make A Way Publications
810 SW 102nd Terrace Unit 101
Pembroke Pines, Florida, 33025
Tel: (305) 988-7031
Email: makeawaypub@gmail.com

*Books will be mailed through regular postal mail media. Delivery may require 2- 3 weeks*

| Quantity | Book Title | Cost | Total |
|---|---|---|---|
| | The Step Before Death $14.99 | $ | |
| Add | U.S Add $4, Outside US $10 Shipping & Handling per book | | |
| | Total Submitted | | |

| Ship to | |
|---|---|
| Name: | |
| Address: | |
| City, State and ZIP | |
| Telephone No.: | |
| Email Address: | |

Thank you for your business!

164

www.ingramcontent.com/pod-product-compliance
Lightning Source LLC
Chambersburg PA
CBHW032031050726
47590CB00006B/2378